Legends of Thamaturga

By: H.C. MacDonald

Cover Art by Laina Vanderwell

HC MacDonald

Copyright © 2016 HC MacDonald

All rights reserved.

ISBN:1539734145
ISBN-13: 9781539734147

DEDICATION

Thank you to all my fans. I hope you like this next adventure.

Kate, Liz & John, I love you. You inspire me.

Ryan, without your encouragement and support I wouldn't have done this. Thank you.

Special Thanks to Laina Vanderwell for creating a great cover and Lillian Osborne High School.

HC MacDonald

Legends of THAMATURGA The Contestant

CONTENTS

Prologue

1	Plans	1
2	Invitation	9
3	Reunion	22
4	Hope	39
5	Obstacle	52
6	Koboldrone	64
7	Awaken	78
8	Ankylynx	82
9	Sleep	91
10	Confused	98
11	Round Three	102
12	Adjustment	108
13	Announcement	117
14	Contract	126
15	Duggars	135
16	Deception	161
17	Interview	175
18	Discovery	181
19	Labyrinth	192
20	Decision	200
21	Divide	206
22	Forward	217
23	Dream	233
	Sneak Peak Book 4	239

HC MacDonald

Prologue

The plan had begun. The cloaked man moved about the crowded streets unnoticed by the other villagers. He was collecting information. Now that the war was over, villagers talked openly with him of magic, unafraid of the consequences.

He entered the room of a bald fat man sitting on the edge of a hay cot bed. The man looked him in the eye.

"I knew you would come, I saw it in my dreams."

"You know then what I will do to you."

"I do not have the power to stop you, but I have foreseen the one who does."

"Soon I will foresee it. Change it, and you will still be dead."

He stepped toward the man. The man pounded a fist to his chest, in his hand a poison covered dagger. He fell onto the bed. A pool of blood seeping out around him, staining the grey sheets red. Anger steamed from the man in the cloak.

He turned to the unlit fireplace and with a ball of fire lit the wood in the hearth. He reached down and grabbed a burning twig. Before the man on the bed could take his last breathe he was branded.

The silver milky snake slithered out of the mans ear and toward the cloaked figure. It wrapped up his arm and into his hood. As the man on the bed exhaled his final breath, the snake disappeared.

The cloaked man threw the stick violently into the fire. "I will find another." Then he disappeared.

Part 3

The Contestant

lans
Raina

It had been three years since Nezra had died. Peace befell onto the land. I should have been happy. I wasn't. I was still heartbroken over Leon. Alastair said it would take time. Our kind loved deeply. Having my family around made it easier. My only reminders, were when Sanna would visit. I loved our gatherings, but the gossip, Leon. Would prove to be to much sometimes. Making me ache all over for him.

I spent most of my days learning from Alastair. He shared his story with me. When I was in my mother's womb, he had traveled to the Island that gave his father magic. He asked to have it taken away. The magic was released from his grasp. He watched as the magic burst into rays of light then traveled out into the distance. He didn't realize then, what had happened. In releasing it, the magic needed to find a new vessel. I was chosen. When my mother gave birth to me, I inherited not only my grandfathers magic, but a new line of magic was formed.

Alastair traveled back to island asked that I not be given this burden. He would take it back. It was to late.

The magic was bound to me. He asked to able to retain his knowledge on the workings of using the magic. For years he begged and pleaded with them. They eventually granted him the favor. When he returned back again from the island, we were gone.

My recovery was slow. My fight with Nezra had altered my magical abilities. My broken bones and battle scars were not affected by the many potions and healing lotions applied. I had to let my body heal naturally. I was covered in scars from head to toe. The brands on my leg and arm were altered as well. Not even Alastair new what they meant. We tried removing them again, but had no luck.

Magically, I could do nothing more than parlor tricks. I could change my appearance. I could see the true appearance of anything magically altered. That was about it, no more moving about the land in a blink of an eye. No more spoken or silent spells cast. No more protection walls, or bubbles. I no longer dreamed of visions of my mother or the future. This was frustrating.

With my slow recovery, I was also unable to look for my mother. Alastair had sent scouts around the land to look for her. The relayed to them of my visions of her in a cave by the seashore, as well as the other visions I had of her.

They searched the entire shoreline of all of Thamaturga. No sign of her. Robyn had tried many times with her potions to receive a vision. She also had no luck. We only felt she was still alive. Alastair said that our instincts would know.

Now, after three years, I was stronger. Almost completely back to my old non magic self. I would run every morning to build my strength. Then I would continued to train and perfect my battle skills. The afternoons I spent with Robyn and Alastair. Trying to bring back my magic. I was frustrated, depressed and my heart was not in it. I put on a good front for everyone's benefit. I was tired of them asking if I was okay or how I was feeling. I missed my mom. I missed Leon. I even missed my magic. I was depressed. There was nothing anyone could do about it.

I needed to get away, and wanted desperately to help search for my mother. Alastair had told me of the islands of magic. I had a plan to search for her there. I was saving up enough money for buy passage to the islands. I was having troubles finding anyone that would go there. There were too many superstitions about the islands. Sailors were spooked. At the rate I was making money it would be another few years before I would have a large enough amount to bribe them to go. This just depressed me more.

I worked in the evenings and weekends at the village market, watching over Robyn's booth of potions and powders. Taking orders, selling goods, making deliveries when required. It was a tedious and mind boring job. If I was to look for my mother, a necessary one.

The children were all in school now. With Alastair and Robyn's help, easy to manage and care for. They were happy and carefree. The way a child should be.

I sat at my small wooden booth, hiding from the sun. Staring at the people walking by looking at the wares available in the small market. My thoughts lost in my head. My eyes had been focused for some time on a loose string in the seam of my skirt, when I heard the clearing of a throat. I stood and lifted my head to see a tall broad sandy haired young man looking at me. He was holding a bottle in his hand. He had a chiseled face, and soft blue eyes that sparkled when he smiled. I could feel my cheeks heat up. I quickly looked down again.

"What does this do?" He asked in a husky voice.

"That one is used for animals, settles there stomaches when sick." I answered shyly. I looked up at him again. His smile wide on his face, eyes looking straight at me. "What are you in need of?" I asked trying to stop myself from blushing.

"Do you have anything for scars?" He asked.

"Not today, but I can have some made for you and bring it tomorrow." Hopeful I would see him again.

"Sounds good. What time should I come by?"

"After four and I will have it."

He smiled again and winked this time. "See you then." I felt the heat rush to my cheeks. My hands moving up to cover the red I could feel. What was happening? I sat back down, watching him sander away. A smile lifted the corner of my lips. What was I thinking? Then again, maybe it would be a good distraction from my misery. He was so different from Leon. Leon?! I could feel the depression and guilt nudge at my mind. I looked down the street, the man no longer in view. A smile lit my lips. I let hope sneak in to nip out the depressing thoughts.

I let myself daydream about this stranger till the market closed. Happy to have something else to think about.

I headed home, stopping off to give Robyn the orders for tomorrow night. She eyed me from the side. "Something's different about you?"

"What do you mean?" I asked.

"I don't know, you seem lighter, happier. I can't quite put a finger on it."

I knew what it was, but wasn't about to share. I quickly made an excuse and left for grandfather's. The night was uneventful. Sleep was hard to come. My mind wondered from Leon to the stranger and back again.

Morning came. I took the children to school than began my jog. I needed to let out my anxiety and let my mind relax. I ran for hours. When I got back to the house, Alastair was waiting.

"Your late for practice!" He scolded. He was more worried than angry. I could see. I gave him an apologetic smile and began working on my spells. I would repeat words with Alastair, working to move objects. Nothing would happen. We spent a good hour at it. Then we shifted to potions. Again, mixing, casting, nothing would work. It reminded me of my attempts to mimic my mother. At that thought, my heartache would return.

It was time to head to the market. My shift would be starting soon. I practically skipped all the way there. Eager to engage in another encounter with the man from yesterday. Robyn was waiting for me. That curious look on her face.

"I got it." I almost sang. Not catching myself fast enough.

"You sure you're okay." She looked at me suspiciously.

"Yes, now I know you have things to do, so go on. I got this. Do it everyday, remember." I realized I was talking to much. I couldn't help myself. The harder I tried to look normal, the worse it was. After close to twenty minutes, Robyn finally walked away. Looking over her shoulder a few times before she rounded the curve in the path towards her home.

I waited anxiously, a giddiness to my impatience. I don't know why I was so nervous, I had fought Nezra, been in the arena with a Snapper, fended off all sorts of beasts. Here I was nervous. I kept wiping my hands on my skirt, the sweat building making them clammy. It was now four in the evening, my anxiety was bubbling over. I kept watch up and down the street.

As customers came, I hurried them along, not giving in to conversation. I wanted the booth to be empty when he came. Give us a chance to talk without interruption.

I saw him at the top of the street. He was in a group headed my way. I ran my hands down my skirt to straighten it, then did a quick flip of my hair. I hoped I looked all right. He came to the booth and gave me a smile. I could feel my cheeks blush as I smiled back at him. I reached for the potion. Holding it out, "Here is your request."

"How much do I owe you?" He reached out and placed his hand on mine for longer than needed when taking the potion.

"Ten dafners please." I couldn't meet his eyes. My cheeks still heated from his first smile. I watched his hands as he pulled out the money and handed it to me. As he did, he held my hand for a moment. I looked up to his face.

"Thank you, my wife and I thank you for your help." He winked once more and turned to leave.

I felt my body sag. Married. I should have known better than to get my hopes up. That was my life. Those that knew me before, distrusted me, looked at me with anger and hate. Those that didn't know me, saw only my scars and marks. They looked at me with pity. I, for a moment, thought he would like me. The depression came back. He was showing me pity. In that moment, I felt ugly and worthless.

I spent the rest of my shift sitting on my stool feeling sorry for myself. When the time came to close, I gathered our things and walked dragging my feet to Robyn's to drop off the orders. I went straight to bed when I arrived home. Here I wanted to stay. Locked in my room.

Invitation
Raina

Life was bleak and grey to me. I began sleeping in later and later everyday. My runs longer and longer when I did go out. I wanted to be left alone. I no longer worked on my magic. I didn't see the point. At the market, I kept to myself. My hope, to be as invisible as possible.

One evening when I was headed to my room after work, Alastair mentioned Sanna would be coming for a few days. I felt my stomach flip. I had mixed feelings about the visit. I didn't feel like seeing anyone and at the same time, I wanted her to come. Most of all, I didn't want to hear about Leon. I had wanted to tell her it wasn't a good time, but grandfather already insisted she come.

I spent the next few days in bed. Not even getting out to go to work, I was dreading the visit. The day was here for Sanna to arrive. The kids were playing at a neighbors. I had gotten up with them in the morning and now lay in my bed taking advantage of there absence. I heard the knock on the door and the muffled sound of voices. Then my door burst open and Sanna plopped herself onto my bed slapping my leg as she did.

"Get your lazy but up."

"I don't want to."

"To bad! I hear you been moping around this place. You need to get out of here. Get a change of scenery."

"What are you talking about? I don't need a change of scenery."

"Really, these walls are growing mold from your stink. I'm talking about dancing and meeting new men, and dressing up."

"No! Absolutely not! I don't feel like a party."

"To bad. I already RSVP'd for you. So you are coming."

"No, you can't make me go."

"I can and I will. Besides, Alastair said he would help if I needed him. Come on. Raoul will be there. Robyn is going. You need to come to."

"I can't, who will watch the kids. I can't leave them alone with Alastair. He can't keep up with them. What about my job? Who will tend the market?"

"First, I have it all covered so no excuses. I figured you would try to get out of it. Ethel will watch all the kids, her and Sasha are already at the school waiting to pick them up, and Robyn's okay with the store being closed for a few days while she's gone. Now get up."

"You brought Ethel with you." I said exasperated. It was bad enough to have Sanna here ordering me about, but Ethel too. They would surely gang up on me and I would have no choice but to go.

"Yes, I brought Ethel with me, I needed reinforcements. Anyway, Ethan is waiting for us."

"Oh, in that case, NO!" I yelled.

"Tough! The children were to excited about seeing each other. I am not taking that away from them. You are coming! Whether you like it or not, I am packing your things and dragging you back."

"Back, you mean to Ladow? I can't go back there, to many memories. I can't handle it."

"You need to work this out. I am giving you tough love and making you face your ghosts. If I was in danger would you shy away. No, you would not. You would go running into battle. You need to move forward. This will help you. Now where is your bag."

I sat in bed watching her grab my belongings. She then turned to me, "You have five minutes then I drag you all the way to Ladow."

I knew she would. Stubborn she was. Always got her way. I fell out of bed and threw something on from off my floor. I was ready. I would go, but I wouldn't be happy. She could make me be there, but I didn't have to participate. We headed out the door only to run into Ethel.

"You look terrible. Sanna you didn't tell me you looked this bad. This will not do. You don't have much time to get her ready. You may have to ask them to postpone a day or two."

"Thanks Ethel, I missed you too." I said sarcastically. She hugged me and winked at Sanna. What were they up to? This would be fun, not.

We traveled to Ladow. Ethan talking to me of all the new changes the council had made. Sanna telling me the latest gossip. Ethan inquired of my powers and healing. I explained I still didn't have them. It was a mystery. Alastair and Robyn could not figure it out. They had gone thru every record of my ancestry to uncover the change and how to put things back in harmony. They had no luck. So I demonstrated my few parlor tricks along the way. Ethan was still impressed.

"So, you can't just disappear like before." He asked, looking at Sanna.

"No, I get around like everyone else these days." I rolled my eyes as I said it.

"That's to bad. So if you ran into Leon, you couldn't up and leave. You would have to walk out the door like us?" He continued.

"Yes, that is correct. Why? Why would I run into him? I realize he may be at the dance, but I thought I would be able to avoid him, like I try to do with you all." I said with a sarcastic smile.

"Well, the party is for Leon. So, you may run into him." Ethan said, as he ducked from the punch I threw at his head.

"You should have told me. I wouldn't have come. I don't want to see him." I yelled. Upset at this trick. How could my friends do this to me?

"Well, to be perfectly clear, it is a betrothal ceremony for Leon." Sanna said hiding behind Ethan.

"I can't believe this. I can't go. I can't see him with someone else. I'm not ready for that." I slumped down in my seat of the carriage and sat with my head down and hands folded in my lap. Emotions welling up. It hurt. I knew he was seeing someone, but this. It hurt. I would rather not of known.

Sanna moved next to me and put her arm around me. "You still love him, don't you."

"Yes. Don't make me do this." I pleaded with her. "Just turn around and take me back home."

She kept her arm there. I could here them talking in their wolf language. Due to my changes, my branded shoulder no longer worked either. I coward into myself thinking of Leon, I didn't want to him to see me with all these scars even though I knew it wouldn't matter. He hated me then, I doubted that changed. Before the war, he looked at me with disgust, now with the scars, I knew it wouldn't be much different. I didn't think I could handle the look of hate and pity from him.

We arrived in Ladow. I followed them back to their home. Keeping myself hidden in my hooded cloak. The paths were empty, I was happy not to run into anyone else. When we arrived, I was escorted to Sasha's room. I laid down on the bed, threw her blanket over my head and quietly sobbed to myself. I didn't want to be around anyone. My mind was turning. Slowly I let myself sleep.

It was past noon when I strolled out of Sasha's room. Ethan and Sanna were in the kitchen talking. Both stopped to look at me as I wondered over.

"This is not going to do!" Sanna started.

I held up my hand to stop her. I didn't want to hear what she had to say. I would head back in the next caravan. That was that. Before I could tell her my plan, Ethan gently pulled my hand down to the counter. I looked up to stare into Sanna's eyes.

"You are not this person. You are a strong willed, vibrant woman. What happened to you? You would never let anything as trivial as a loss of magic put you down! This needs to stop now!" She let go of my arm and walked into the main room. Ethan put his arm around my shoulders and gently pushed me behind her.

"A lot has happened, you don't understand." I softly said back at her.

Sanna turned on her heels and grabbed my shoulders. "Don't understand? Don't understand? How can you say that? I have had my share of disappointments and death. You do not get to tell me I don't understand. You made Leon forget you, so don't pity yourself." She let go of my shoulders and blowing out an exasperated breath she was holding sat on the chair.

Ethan gently sat me across from her and went to stand behind Sanna. I felt as if I was about to be interrogated.

Ethan began in a matter of fact voice, "We have allowed you for over two years now to wallow in self pity. But no more! You have a chance to win him back."

My eyes widened at the statement, "I don't want him back."

"Nonsense! You love him and have been pining over him ever since. There are things you need to know. You will listen to me with no interruptions. You will do as I say!"

He stood firm. Arms folded, eyes unblinking. I felt as if I was being scolded by my father. I knew they had my best interests at heart, but that didn't stop the pain and heartache of his betrayal, or the vulnerability I felt from my weaknesses and scars. I sat unmoving, unspeaking with my head hung down looking at the rug on the floor. I waited for him to finish speaking.

Ethan pulled a chair closer to me and lifted my head so our eyes met. "Leon has chosen a mate. Our traditions do not allow for him as chief to be able to choose his wife. There is a challenge that must be met by his chosen and all eligible candidates."

I didn't understand. I didn't care. He had chosen, what did it matter. There could be a hundred other candidates, but if he singled out someone already, then it didn't matter. I remembered the last ceremony. I shook my head out of his hand. Let my eyes drift down to the rug. I needed to not care. It hurt less that way.

"She doesn't understand." Sanna mentioned to Ethan. "You need to be clearer."

"Raina, look. There is a series of challenges all potential mates to the chief must go through. You are signed up to participate."

At those words he stood and stepped behind his chair. My head flew up to look at him, then at Sanna. How could they do this to me? Sign me up. Sanna jumped in to explain further.

"We know you still love him. This is your chance to win him back."

"He hates me. Why would I want to win someone who has obviously chosen someone else? To what, torture myself for the rest of my life. Be with someone who wants somebody else? Why did you do this? I was trying to forget him." I put my head in my hands and tried to keep my tears in check.

"Because, we think he still loves you. We think something else happened that night. We need more time." Sanna pleaded.

"Why do you think that?" I asked looking from one to the other.

Ethan began pacing. Sanna began talking to him again in their language. "Stop! Stop with the secrets, just tell me already." My anger coming to the forefront.

Ethan began explaining again, "Three women are chosen to compete for his hand. One Leon chooses, one the council chooses and one that wins the village challenge. We need you to win."

"I still don't understand. If he has chosen, then why the others, why would he want to be married to someone not of his choice." It didn't make sense. None of it did.

It was Sanna's turn to talk and explain. "The women he has chosen wears your necklace. Partly why we think something else is going on. Why we need time."

"I don't understand, I don't have a necklace. What does it have to do with his betrayal?" My head was starting to hurt. Nothing made any sense. It all seemed like more heartbreak for me. If chosen, I would get to see his disgust of me daily, if not chosen, I would get to live with the thought of him with another. I was at a loss either way. I rubbed my temples working to release the pressure building up.

Sanna began explaining again. "You don't understand. At the wedding years ago, you wore a necklace, an enchanted pendant. Do you remember?" She waited for my response.

"Yes, what about it?" I said with a little more anger than I wanted to come out.

"Leon took your necklace, right." Her eyebrow rose and she waited for my confirmation.

"Yeah, so, he pulled it off my neck, and walked off, disgusted that it was me." My head was really starting to pound.

"He took it to claim you as his own."

"You don't look at someone the way he did to claim them." I retorted.

"He was surprised by the revelation. No one has ever chosen a mate outside our people. His natural reaction is to hide his feelings, hide his emotions. It was a time when any emotion was a weakness that Erebos would try to exploited." She paused to look at me.

"He told us he loved you. He went that morning to bring you and the children back. It was his idea to rescue you at the fortress. His idea to be captured." Ethan said.

"I still don't see how that matters. Things changed. He wanted me to be owned by the village, enslaved. You don't do that to someone you love." My head felt on fire. The pounded now making me nauseated. I stood to head back to Sasha's bed. Ethan walked over and pushed me back down in my chair.

"My head hurts." I said quietly. I looked down at the rug trying to will the pounding between my ears away. Ethan left and returned with some powder and water. "Take this, it will ease your headache." He handed me the cup. I took the medicine.

I closed my eyes waiting for the pounding to subside. Waiting for them to explain why I needed to be here. After a few minutes Sanna began talking again. "I know you don't understand. You must trust us. Your necklace has your scent, your essence. If Lace is wearing it, then she smells like you. I don't know how she got it, but she did. If he chose her, he is choosing you."

I looked up at her. Shook my head. I didn't understand. "You might be mistaken. Everyone had those necklaces. Besides, I'm sure there are other things besides smell as to why he chose her. I don't think it matters."

Sanna and Ethan both let out an exasperated breath of air.

"You're not getting it. She stole your necklace. He still has feelings for you. She is playing with him." She was standing, now adamant to get her point across. "Don't you see, subconsciously he is choosing you. We think it is his way to regain his memories of you. He doesn't realize it, but he wants you."

"His return of memories will not erase the fact that he would rather have me as a slave." I yelled at them, my frustration hitting a peak. "I don't care that he may still love me somehow. He betrayed me. He begged me to be you all's slave. He did that. Would you forgive Ethan if he wanted you enslaved. To live your life in a prison cell. I was there. I lived it for ten years. How could he want that for me, for my life? So what if he does remembers. Great, now he can remind everyone that they can use me as they wish, lock me back up."

I stormed out of the room, twisting my arm out of Ethan's grip as he tried to stop me. I walked out the front door, slamming it behind me and took off running. I needed to get away from them all. Clear my head. I took off down the path that ran the outskirts of the South border. No one lived down this way. I knew I could be alone.

Reunion
Leon

The challenge was to begin in a few days. My anxiety was growing. Lace was beautiful. Her long black hair was silky to the touch. Her skin a light olive, giving her a glowing shine. Her eyes a deep grey. Reminding me of storm clouds in the summer. She was slender and tall, walked with a sway that would turn the heads of any man. Her smile, mysterious and intriguing. She was so delicate.

We spent most of our time together. I had met her a year or so ago. I was coming back from the meadow deep in thought, when I came across her in the middle of my path. She had sprained her ankle and was sitting on a rock in the path nursing her foot. I carried her back to my home. There, I cared for her till she was able to move about again.

I normally didn't care for the damsel in distress attitude. As chief I needed a strong female that could handle herself. Someone like my sister, self sufficient, yet endearing and selfless. Lace could be like that if she wanted. She was not self sufficient, always needed my help, but at times she was kind and endearing. Not to mention beautiful. Her scent was intoxicating. She smelled of a fresh summers day, which gave me the feeling of hope and making me think anything was possible. I couldn't get enough of it.

Before we had met, I had heard of her. She was always described as ambitious, controlling, and high maintenance. She was nothing like that. It was probably just girls jealous of her beauty that made up these rumors. Many times she demanded more of my attention than I could give, but, I wouldn't describe her as high maintenance or controlling. When I was able to assist and catered to her I would find it intoxicating to be with her, so I didn't mind.

I had been in the meadow strategizing the upcoming challenges. I wanted her to win. As chief, I was bound to our traditions. I could choose a mate to compete, but the challenges would prove her worthy to be my bride. Worthy to protect and care for the village.

Lace would compete against two other nominees. One nominee is chosen by the council. They interview selective candidates in our land. One is chosen by the people via a series of obstacles and tests.

My mother had been a council nominee. My father was instantly attracted to her, they had been in love ever since. Together they were a charitable, kind, powerful couple.

The people's nominee is usually one of our strong women warriors. Because it is open participation, any one of any origin can participate. We even at times get females from other villages and packs. However, the way the obstacles are set up only a shifter could win the games. Most outsiders didn't make it past the first challenge.

In essence the games were more of a show of politics and peace. Allowing for our allies to participate. This time the first game was an obstacle course. Using a series of paths through the village, a variety of obstacles were set up. This showed agility and speed. The top half of the group would move on.

The second game was tougher. The remaining participants had to spend the night in a Ankylynxs' cage. It is a catlike creature with a spotted coat of fur and nail like spikes on the end of its long thin tail. It's cuddly appearance was marred by its bad temper, sharp teeth, and long clawed paws. It's screams would make any man fear the dark. It was no taller then my knee, but quick as lightning. Most only heard the screams it made not fast enough to see it before it would attack. It could hide in the crevasses of the rocks. At night, became virtually invisible, sneaking up on its pray and attacking with its long spiked tail and teeth.

Each women would have to protect themselves from midnight to sunrise the next day. Because of the dangerous nature of these creatures one could ring out of the competition. Most candidates did. Trainers were also stationed to ensure everyone's safety. If the woman got in a situation she could not handle, the trainer would rescue her from the beast. The candidates would have to wait till sunrise to find out if they moved on. Usually, everyone rang out, and they would take the top five women who lasted the longest to move on.

The last game was the hardest. Not to be discriminative, but it was purposely meant to differentiate our kind from any others. We took a small enchanted object and magnified its scent. The object under the enchantment would change its appearance throughout the game, but would keep the same scent. It is shown in a different form to all the seekers. The object is then hidden, and the game begins.

The seekers must find the object, however, you can only find it by scent. Hence, a shifter with our natural heightened ability would be able to sniff it out. It becomes a race between shifters to get to the object. No other kind has ever been able to find the object. They find themselves looking for something that was not there. Only the finder of the item wins and becomes the nominee.

I wasn't worried about who would win the games. I knew most of the other women in the village. Rarely did a shifter from outside join in the games. Lace had enough skills to beat anyone that made it to the challenges. The nominee would be no match for the others. I began thinking about the upcoming challenges Lace would face.

The first challenge the three women would face would be the 'Duggers'. These were nasty little razor sharp feathered creatures that would nip at your ankles. Roughly a foot long in length, but could jump a good two feet high. They were quick and could balance on any size rope or beam. The course was held in the arena that replaced our ceremonial grounds for the time.

A series of ropes and beams would stretching the length of the arena. Creating a web of dead ends, pitfalls, and high ropes. The duggers are set loose on the course. Each person would have to navigate from their starting platform to a colored compliment platform on the other side of the arena. Without falling off. This was key. It didn't matter if you were stung by a dugger, as long as you stayed on the course, or were not the first to fall. The first to land in the netting was eliminated, the challenge over.

I had been working with Lace on her balance skills. She struggled on the ropes when required to jump over the fake dugger obstacles I had created. We had strategized her to stay on the wood beams, not worry about the platform. This way, she would keep her balance when jumping over duggers. Most likely one of the other two candidates would make the fatal error on the ropes and land in the net. Lace would then move on to an easier challenge for her.

The second game was a more strategic. A series of mazes and labyrinths would be assembled. Each nominee would need to find there way out. The Elders would add tests and challenges along the way. No one but the Elders knew what they were. I worked with Lace on her speed, agility, and ability to recall where she had been. Lace had no internal compass. She could not find her north from her south. Let alone figure out where she had been. Together we worked on ways to mark her path. This she could do. As for the challenges, we worked on various fighting skills, mental games, and strategy. Hopefully, this would be enough for her to make it to the end. That was my goal. Do what I could to get her there. If she made it to the end, then, we could announce our engagement and begin the plans for our wedding day.

That couldn't come fast enough. The Council had begun hounding me regularly to start the process, of finding a mate. Giving up my bachelorhood was not something I was looking forward to. I couldn't imagine myself settled down, starting a family right now. There were still things to do.

I wanted to search out the land for the remaining Raiders that had retreated. There were rumors brewing in the south of a new threat. I wanted to investigate. I didn't have time to play housemate. Then there would be Lace. She wouldn't want to travel with me. I loved her, but I valued my independence. When this was all done, we would have to figure out how to make it work.

I sat up from my spot in the meadow where I had been laying, thinking about what was to come. I closed my eyes and took in a few deep breaths. I could smell someone coming my way. I inhaled a deep breath through my nose, letting the scent resinate. Lace. She was coming headed down the side path that rounded towards Sanna's home. I closed my eyes, leaned back onto the grass, and let the scent drift toward me. I could never smell her this far off before. Usually her scent was very faint. I could only smell it when we were close to each other. Maybe the fact that I could smell it now was my way of admitting that I had allowed myself to love her. Awakening my inner beast to her scent. I still had my hesitations of her, but I would allow them no longer to block my senses.

I heard her footsteps. They were lighter than normal, not quite the same. Maybe she was trying to sneak up on me. I thought with a smile. We had worked on it, but today, she was the quietest she had ever been. I pretended to be napping as to not spoil the illusion. She was moving toward me. Then stopped. I waited, trying hard not to spoil her surprise. Anticipation curled inside me. Her scent so intoxicating. I was having trouble holding myself back from grabbing her leg and pulling her down with me. I listened. Her smell, flowing all around me. Then it began drifting, further away. I waited, unsure as to what she was doing. I listened for footsteps. Nothing. I opened my eyes and sat up. There, at the edge of the meadow was not Lace, but the wizard girl from the war all those years ago. I could feel my face harden. I looked around for Lace. She was no where in site.

"What did you do with her?" I demanded to the girl as she was running away on the path. When she didn't look back or slow down, I got up and took off running toward her. She was quick. I took off into the woods a shortcut for the path she was running on. I could get in front of her and cut her off at the boulder. She was going to tell me what she did with Lace.

I made it to the boulder. I took in a few deep breaths to slow my heart rate. I focused on the scents of the forest. There coming my direction, was Lace's scent. It was either Lace or this trick. I heard the soft sound of a branch snap. She was turning into the woods. I moved from behind the boulder.

"Where do you think you're going?" I asked, startling her to a stop.

She looked at me. Tears running down her face. She turned her back to me for a moment and when she looked back, her face had no emotion. For a moment I felt compassion for her, but, only a moment. She was after all, a wizard. Even though others had praised and welcomed her, she was still not to be trusted. "Where is Lace?" I questioned.

"What?!" She looked confused at my question.

"You were in the meadow, so was my girlfriend. What did you do with her?" I could feel my anger begin to stir.

"I don't know what you are talking about. When I ran through, you were the only one I saw. Maybe, she went somewhere." She turned at that and went to walk away.

"So, you think I should believe you?" I said sarcastically.

"Yeah!" she raised her voice at me. "Yeah, I do. I have never done anything to make you think otherwise. I do not betray people." She took a step forward.

Something was wrong here, I couldn't figure it out. I took a step in her direction. As I went to speak, heard another snap of a twig from behind the boulder.

I turned in time to see Lace walk around the path. She looked at me and then at the girl. Then with a graceful stride, was to my side, wrapping her arms around my neck and pulling me into a heated kiss. I watched the girl as I kissed Lace. For a moment, I thought I saw a tear run down her face. She had turned her back to me. I barely heard the whisper that escaped her mouth as she ran into the woods. "I don't betray those I love like you do."

What was she talking about? I pulled Lace off me and held her at arms length. I looked at her. My mind puzzled for a moment.

"Where were you?" I asked. Still holding onto her shoulders.

"Silly, I went to meet you. I saw you leave the meadow, so I took the shortcut to the path. It worked cause her you are." She batted her eyes, and pouted her lips, making me feel bed. "What was she doing here?" She asked stiffly.

"My fault darling. I thought she was causing trouble. You know how they are. Can't trust them." I gave Lace a half smile and ran my hand in my hair. I was feeling guilty for accusing the girl of taking Lace. She must have been crossing the meadow when I smelled Lace coming. The winds, had probably turned her scent from me, causing me to think she was leaving. It all made sense. If I was a bigger man, I would apologize, but chances were, the girl would cause trouble anyway. I would need to speak with Sanna, see what she knows, find out why she is here. Sanna, knows all the gossip in the village. If anyone could find out, it would be her.

I smiled down at Lace who had wrapped her arms around my chest. She was very possessive. Sometimes, that was attractive, but right now, I found it annoying.

I pushed her back, took her hand and lead her down the path toward the market. "Are you ready for tomorrow?" I inquired.

"Yes." She answered and laid her head on my shoulder. "Why is she here?"

"I don't know. I plan to investigate. In the meantime," I kissed her forehead, "don't let her bother you. I will see she is asked to leave."

Lace lifted her head and smiled, "See that you do."

We hit a fork in the path. She pulled me close and gave me a long lingering kiss. Then I watched as she swayed away into the curve of the path. She was quite the temptress when she wanted to be. I shook my head and let my smile widen. Then turned and headed toward Sanna's.

I arrived at Sanna's, knocked on the door before walking in. Not waiting for them to answer. Ethan came out of the side room. The look of surprise written on his face quickly changed to a stern look.

"What brings you here Leon?" Ethan stated. Not as friendly as he usually was.

"Well, I was looking for my sis. Is she here?" I looked around the home, no sign of Sasha or Sanna.

"She is occupied at the moment, but I will have her call on you when she is free." He walked toward me, then past me to the door, where he opened it and stood to usher me out.

"I can wait." I walked over to the chair, ignoring his polite suggestion to leave. I wanted some answers. I could wait. There little tiff was no concern of mine. The ceremonies were tomorrow, I wanted to know nothing was going to happen.

"She'll be awhile, you know with all that's going on tomorrow. I will have her ring you." He stood firm by the door, unmoving.

"Say, have you heard anything about that wizard being in the village?" I figured if Sanna knew, he may to.

She wasn't much for keeping secrets or gossip from Ethan. Besides, what was his deal. He needed to relax. If they were fighting, then kicking me out wasn't going to help. I would just keep coming back till I got my answers. I watched Ethan as he moved uncomfortably by the door. He knew something, I could tell. "What do you know?" I pushed for an answer.

"If you are referring to Raina, yes she is here. Other than that," he let out a sigh, "there is nothing more I can tell you." He looked angry. Why, I didn't know. He had changed a few years back, right after the war. We no longer joked as much and he really didn't like Lace.

"Why?" I asked, not moving from my chair.

"Look, you can't stay. I have things to do." His face hardened toward me and the stern look he gave me told me he wasn't going to share anything else. Why I didn't know. I stood and walked to the door. Before stepping all the way out, I turned to him, "I will have her removed from the village you know."

Ethan grabbed my shoulder hard and gave me a shove out the door. "If you know what's best for you, you will leave Raina alone." Then he slammed the door shut.

What was his problem? Leave her alone, no, she would leave us alone. I strolled to the market to see what else I could find out. Ethan would be of no help.

It was late in the afternoon, my inquiries in the village now done. I headed to the grounds to help. The arena now stood tall and ready for the week ahead. The obstacles set up for the first event. Tomorrow, the games would begin. I was tired. I laid on my bed, hoping to catch a few hours of sleep before the festivities kicked off tonight. It was only a dinner and dance to start the event, but, I would be required to entertain and dance with most of the contestants, even if they didn't make it past the first round. It would be exhausting. I tried not to think of it. My mind relaxed and I drifted to sleep.

I awoke to a slap on my back. "Who do you think you are?" Sanna yelled at me.

"What?" I was still waking myself up. My mind foggy. My eyes filled with sleep. Sanna slapped me again. "Who do you think you are?"

"You do that again and I will slap you back Sanna. Don't think I won't." I rubbed my lower back where the sting from her slap resided. "What are you talking about?" I sat up to look at her.

She was seething mad. I could almost see the smoke coming out of her ears. Again, what was her deal. Whatever fight her and Ethan got in was now falling onto me. Sanna began stomping around the room, opening and slamming drawers, chests, huffing and puffing.

"You..You think you are so smart...You think can just treat anyone anyway you want. Well, I told mom and she is coming soon. And you are going to hate yourself for the way you are acting." She began storming out of my room and toward the front door. I jumped off my bed to head her off.

"What are you talking about?" I had her by the shoulders with my back on the front door. "What ever it is your wrong. Got the wrong guy."

"I highly doubt that your chieftain." She said with over dramatic wave of her hand.

"Seriously, what are you talking about. Come on, tell me what's going on."

"Why do you hate her so much?" Sanna let her head hang down and she moved to sit in the chair by the fire. "Why are you so mean to her?"

"Who are you talking about? I'm not mean to anyone. I treat everyone with respect and kindness." I was kneeling in front of her, hands on her knees. I wanted to understand what was going on with my sister. What was wrong so I could fix it?

"Raina." Sanna looked me square in the eyes when she said it. I felt a pang of guilt. I didn't like her. I didn't trust her. I hated the idea of who she was. It was my turn to look at the floor. I moved to the chair opposite of her and ran my hand in my hair.

"Why is this wizard so important to you?" I asked, not fully understanding her emotions.

"Her name is Raina. You knew it once."

"Maybe I did, maybe I didn't, but she is not to be trusted."

"You don't know what you're talking about Leon."

"Really, I think I do. We have been at war for years fighting her kind. Now you want to side with one. How are they different? How is 'Raina' different? She will betray you the moment her power is questioned. Then we will be at war again, only this time with a younger version."

"No, you are wrong. If you would remember, you would not think like that. Do not make her leave." She pleaded with me.

"I don't want her mischief around. This is important to me Sanna." I pleaded back.

"I can vouch for her, she will not cause any harm. Your process will go on as planned." I could see the hint of a mischievous glint in her eye. She was up to something.

"Sanna, no troubles. Everything the way it should be." I tried to convince her.

"Sure thing brother, everything the way it should be. Got it." She was a little to happy. "Oh, by the way do you still have that locket you took from the maiden at Courtney and Brennon's wedding?" a sly smile crossed her lips.

"You know I don't. Fell out of my pocket at the wedding. Besides, I never pursued her. My feelings are for Lace. She is the one I am drawn to, my choice! Not some random person. If that person had been the one…" now it was my turn to be sarcastic, "…I would have searched for her. You know how it works." I shook my head, sisters, I didn't understand them.

"I have to go. Things to do you know. Everything as it should be." She smiled and gave me a peck on the cheek then skipped out the door. Trouble just left my home. Its name was Sanna. She was definitely up to something.

Hope
Raina

I don't know how I got talked into doing this, but here I was headed to the opening ceremonies as a participant. Sanna still convinced that Leon loves me. You wouldn't know it by the kiss he planted on his girlfriend. They both had some crazy conspiracy theories. Sanna thinks now that he was tricked into betraying me. She thinks his girlfriend is enchanting him somehow. She thinks he is blinded by the absence of his memories; and here I am insane enough to listen. I guess it has always been my weakness to hope for the impossible. I always have.

So here I am agreeing with her crazy plan. My job, to do the best I can and try to be selected. I had reminded Sanna that Leon wanted me sent out of the village. Ethan reminded her of that to. It's not like I could participate unnoticed. And there was my mistake. Sanna's eyes grew wide and her smile broad and wicked at the idea of me being unnoticed.

Sanna's great idea was me participating as someone else. One of the few things I could do with my magic. Change my appearance. So for the rest of the afternoon she had me trying different physiques to come up with the perfect disguise. I was a healthy, almost plump size woman. Mid length brown hair, and lightly tan skin. My eyes were still blue. I couldn't get them to change for long periods of time so we left them alone. Sanna turned me around a few times and with a clap of her hands, announced we had a winner. I looked at myself in the mirror. I didn't recognize what I saw. A quick blink and I could see my reflection, only now I had a shimmer of pink magic surrounding my body. It would hold. I set the spell in place and the mirage was complete. We entered the main room to show off the new me to Ethan. He agreed it was a great disguise. Only one problem he could see. I still smelled like me. That was definitely going to be a problem!

    I sat on a chair and thought long and hard. I had never tried to change how I smelt. It never occurred to me. I didn't even know if I could do it. I focused on my scent. Eyes closed, slow breaths. I had been like that for over five minutes. Ethan began coughing and sputtering. I opened my eyes to see if he was okay. He was waving his hand in front of his nose. "Did I do it?" I asked excitedly. I honestly didn't know. Ethan only shook his head and left the room.

    Sanna came over to me. Told me to tone it down if I didn't want to kill everyone in the house with the smell of burnt cookies. Odd I thought. I had been thinking of the cookies Keiko had made before I left. I was so depressed we burnt the first batch. I was feeling depressed now. The plan, the idea of winning him back. The thought that Sanna was wrong. I closed my eyes and tried to soften the scent. "That's good there." Sanna said to me. So, again I bound the spell. I was ready for this crazy plan to start. We didn't even know if I would make it past the first game. We had to try. I owed it to myself Sanna had said. I wanted to believe her, so here I was. Standing with a group of women, preparing to fight for my destiny.

All the participants for the games were gathered together in the Council chambers. Here we were instructed on the first event. The obstacle course. It would be fifteen miles around the ceremonial grounds, ending in the arena. Only the fastest would move on. Spotters would be placed around the course in case any one was injured or wanted to ring out. As I listened to the Elder give the instructions, I glanced at the other participants. They were all very attractive, slender, fit women. I caught a few look my way getting frown or laugh from the contestants. It was probably my disguise. I was easily twice the size of any female there. I was beginning to second guess Sanna's choice of physiques. Once the instructions and timeline details were complete, we were dismissed.

I headed back to Sanna's to prepare for the banquet and dance that would kick off the event. I dreaded the thought of seeing Leon. Sanna suggested I take all my anxiety over him and put it into the race. When I reached her home, she was already dressed and waiting for me. This dance didn't require the usual fine enchanted gowns. Instead, Sanna wore a glistening short violet gown. It made her skin shine, eyes sparkle, and her legs long and sleek. She handed me a long thin strapped red sparkling gown. A frown creased my face. "I can't wear this. The other participants already think I'm a joke, this will only show my scars. Is there anything else?" I pleaded to Sanna. She smiled at me. "You are forgetting one thing....you are not you, you are Pearl!" She floated the dress around the room.

"Pearl, have you gone crazy. I am not a pearl."

"Oh, but you are. A burnt cookie smelling, athletically plump, game winner pearl. That is what I am calling you. So, Pearl, are we getting dressed or not?"

I looked to Ethan for support. Nothing. He just shook his head and turned away. I snatched the dress out of her waving hands and went to Sasha's room to change. When I came out, she smiled at me. "See, for Pearl, this is the perfect dress. Very flattering to her tone and body. Now let's do something to your hair and face." I followed her to her room and let her do what she does.

When I looked in the mirror, I looked horrendous. The rouge was to dark, the lipstick to bright. The dress hung loose around my waist. My scars contrasting with the bright silk fabric. The red of the dress washing out my skin making me look ill. No, this was a mistake. I could still back out. I shook my head and turned to leave. Sanna reached out and grabbed my arm. "Look at Pearl, not you." She said sweetly. I blinked my eyes a few times to allow myself to see the magic illusion that was in place. Sanna was right. The gown was flattering. No scars to see. No pale white skin to clash with the color. My face was shadowed in beautiful shades to compliment my skin tone and eyes. Sanna knew how to bring out the best in anyone. I closed my eyes and the illusion was gone. I nodded my approval and together we walked out of her home. Ready to start the night.

    We entered the North side of the village market. It had been transformed into a festival of lights, music, and food. Colorful ribbons and lanterns created an awning over the temporary stone dance floor. Tables with colorful linens and flowers decorated the edge of the stone floor. The Elders sat at a large table overlooking the commotion. Two large wooden chairs sat at the end of the table, empty. According to Sanna these were for the Chief's and Council's nominee's seating places. I looked at the empty chairs. My stomach felt nauseous thinking of the competition ahead. Sanna must have sensed my worry. She put her arm around me and gave me a squeeze. "They won't know what hit them. You got this gal." She dragged me over to a table and began introducing my as Pearl. I couldn't help but laugh to myself. Sanna was so over the top, Ethan and I both were embarrassed. It was Sanna, nothing you could do but love her enthusiasm. By the time the festivities started, our table was team Pearl.

The festivities started with a greeting from the Elders and Leon. Cheers rang out around the crowd. Then Leon announced his nominee, Lace. Again, cheers rang from the crowd. Everywhere but at our table. Sanna was making sure none of them cheered for the other nominees. Either out of fear or fun, they obliged. Ethan and I shared a secret laugh at our companions expense. Leon's nominee was the same woman he had kissed in the woods on my run. She wore a tight short red dress with no back. She was breathtakingly beautiful. Around her neck was a long chain hanging mid waist. Attached was a pendant of some sort. I could see the glow of magic surrounding it. My mind flickered back to Sanna's theories. She could be on to something. Trouble was, with my powers virtually gone, I wouldn't be to solve the mystery that surrounded Lace, or be able to break the memory spell I put on Leon even if I wanted to. It was all up to him to remember on his own.

Next, the nominee from the Council was announced. Again, except for our table who was looking at Sanna to see if they should join in the cheer, which they did not, the audience roared their pleasure. The final announcement was the introduction of the participants in the games. We each stood and filed in a line up to the podium by the Council's table. One by one, each told their name and received cheers from the crowd. As I stepped up, I could see other participants and guests mocking, and making fun of me. I swallowed hard. I knew they didn't see the real me, but it still hurt. I stated my name and my village. A pity clap came from behind me, followed by unenergized cheers, until I heard my table. They were on their feet cheering and hooting. It put the smile back on my face and I felt the heat of embarrassment on my cheeks. I strolled back to my table, and was greeted with cheers and hugs all around. When all the participants were done, the banquet began.

Our table conversation turned to me on strategy, tips, and how unsportsmanlike the crowd had been. It only fueled their loyalty to see me succeed. By the time dinner was over and the dancing began, I knew of three of the obstacles, how to best get through them, and the weaknesses of most the other players. For the first time since hearing this crazy plan, I had confidence I could make it past the first game.

As the dancing proceeded I sat quietly watching the others. Leon was dancing with each nominee and participant. When no one was looking, his date would sneak in a dance and kiss. I didn't want to watch, but couldn't stop. At one point Leon came over toward my table but was cut off by another participant. He never made it back over.

It was getting late in the hour, I wanted to get my rest for the event tomorrow. I had lost sight of Leon and his girlfriend hours ago. I headed into the dancing crowd to find Sanna and Ethan. As I moved between couples, I could hear the snicker of a laugh or rude comment aimed in my direction. It made me sad that they could not accept others for who they were. I finally spotted the two at the far end of the dance floor. I had only taken a few steps when I was stopped by a hand on my shoulder. I turned, braising myself for Leon. It wasn't him. Instead it was Raoul. "May I have this dance?" How could I refuse? He had been my teacher, ally and friend. It had been sometime since I had seen him. I nodded in agreement and took his hand. Together we began dancing. Raoul looked at me with an ounce of recognition, "I hate to impose on you," he began with a hesitation, "but you said you were from Nanton. Do you by any chance know a Raina or Robyn?"

A smile escaped my lips. "Yes, I know them well." I answered back.

"How are they doing?" He inquired further.

"Robyn is doing good. She planned on coming but at the last moment had something else come up. She misses you ya know. Talks about you often."

"Does she?" His face twitched and his cheeks gave way to just a slight hint of a blush. "And Raina? I worry about her."

"She will be all right. I think she has turned a new chapter in her book." I replied shyly.

Raoul was looking at me. "You seem so familiar to me. I hate to forget someone, but have we met?"

A shy smile lifted the corner of my mouth. I looked down to his neck and then back up to his eyes. He squinted at me and I saw the spark of recognition as I let him see through my mirage. He said nothing but pulled me in for a deep embrace. "I applaud your efforts." He was bowing his head as he said it. "I truly wish you both the best of luck. Have you forgiven him for what he has done?"

"I don't know. Sanna seems to think there was something more. A missing peace to why he did what he did. I have decided to have some faith in that."

"Why not just ask him, remove your memory spell and a..s..k..... Oh, you are blocked.... This makes sense .... Robyn wrote to me of your struggles, I just didn't realize how bound you were till I guess now. What are you able to do?"

"You're looking at it. This and the ability to see when magic is used. I can't do anything about it though." It was my turn to hang my head again at the embarrassment of my abilities. Raoul took his hand and lifted my face to look at him again.

"Raina, it is not your ability to use magic that has made you powerful and special. It is the kindness of your heart. The open love you give. You should not be embarrassed of any of your abilities. It was you who lead others from the fortress. It was you who fought off a snapper. It was you who protected those children and countless others, not the magic. You are the same as you were before. Remember that." Raoul stepped back holding me at arms length. "Thank you for the dance." He bowed as a gentleman did. "You are truly a lovely woman." With a wink he walked away.

I stood in the middle of the dance floor. Happy to see my old friend. I began looking around for Ethan and Sanna. They were no longer in the back corner I had spotted them before. I decided they would understand if I left without saying goodbye. I began working my way toward the edge of the dance floor. I was almost home free when I heard a cackle of a laugh. It was Lace, Leon's girlfriend. She walked toward me.

"You may want to rethink showing up tomorrow. Save yourself the embarrassment of coming in last." She snickered out. "Someone like you, will never win a man like him." She nodded in the direction of Leon. I followed her gaze. I could see him watching us. I looked back at her. Noticing the chain on her neck. I scooped up the pendant in my hand. "Interesting necklace choice you have." She ripped the necklace out of my hand and tucked it into the top of her gown out of view. Then turned and stalked away. It was definitively enchanted. I continued walking toward the path.

I had made it half way to Sanna's when I heard the footsteps behind me. I turned to face the person following me. It was Raoul. He was walking quickly, and was upon me in no time. "?Raina??" and he paused.

I laughed. "Yes, it is me."

"Whew, I wasn't sure. I took the liberty to ask around some of the old Council members. I think Sanna has some merit in her theory. Please let her know I will do my best to seek out the answers. If Ethan or Sanna could meet with me at the Atheneum I think we can get some answers." He patted my shoulder and nodded, "It's good to see you out and about again. I have missed my student."

I smiled at Raoul, "I've missed you too. You know, when this is all over, you should come back with me for a short while. Visit with old friends." Now it was my turn to wink at him. His blush returned. He patted me once more and strode away. "Good luck tomorrow Raina, I'm rooting for you."

I knew he was sincere. He had been my only friend more than once in my life. I loved and respected him. I pondered the words he had said. Sanna had merit. Guilt and grief hit me at once. If Sanna was right, then this was my fault as to why he hated me. I was to blame for the betrayal not Leon. If he had been tricked. I was the one to not have faith in him. Not trust him. I was the one who betrayed him. I wanted to cry, the hurt overwhelming me of my mistake. I had to win now. I had to figure out how to get his memories back, then, hopefully he would forgive me for what I had done. I could feel myself withdrawing from the world, the depression coming back ten fold. How could he forgive me for this? I sat on a nearby boulder letting myself be consumed by the guilt.

I don't know how long I sat there, but when I heard the sound of soft giggles and footsteps coming my way, I stood and ran to Sanna's place. In Sasha's room, in silence, I cried myself to sleep. Tomorrow would be a long day.

Morning came quick. I got up, showered, ate, and mentally prepared myself for the race ahead. I could not dwell on the unknown. This was not who I was. Once I let out all my tears last night, I felt better. Today, today I would hope for us. Hope for forgiveness and understanding. Above all, hope that I would make it to round two.

Obstacle
Raina

The starting bell echoed in my ears as I ran down the path in a heard of women. According to my table group team we would be coming up to the first obstacle, the rope swings. These were a series of ropes hung from a long beams of wood over a tar pit. If you fell, you did not get out. I rounded the corner and saw the spectacle. It was long and wide. If I didn't know better I would have thought the rest of the race was just this obstacle. I couldn't see the end of the ropes and tar pit felt miles below. As I blinked, the course shortened, looking more manageable. It was an illusion. This was a mental as well as physical. Already, some of the women backed out due to shear mental defeat.

I stopped at the edge of the pit, trying to assess the distance. My 'team' as I like to say, told me to stay high on the ropes and to move fast. I took the first leap and grabbed high, swinging my body toward the second rope. Hand over hand I swung, following their directions as best I could. I tried not to look at the others, especially when one would slip, scream, and fall. It was distracting. Others were flying by me at a faster pace. I concentrated on my task at hand. My grip getting tired. I missed the rope, and my hand slid down burning my skin. I tightened my grip before I lost the rope altogether, saving myself from falling. Now with two hands on the rope I tried to get my swing back. I was half way across. After a few movements back and forth, I felt confident enough to reach out. I grabbed hold of the rope and again began my swing across. Working to keep my grip tight. I was now at the bottom of the ropes with no room for error.

As I approached the end of the rope test, my team was their cheering me on. Sanna and Ethan were not. I figured they would be with Raoul. We had to know the truth. I hoped they would make it back before the race was over.

I was near the end of the pack. I had some ground to make up. I sprinted to the next obstacle, the rock pillars. I was told to move to the outsides, the pillars were closer together and would be easier to hop across. In the center they would be spaced further apart, causing you to miss your step and fall. Netting was placed halfway down the twenty foot high pillars, ready to catch you. The fall was still terrifying. I ran to the outside set. Began leaping across. Forward, sideways, forward. Moving as quickly as I dared. I was making ground. Moving faster than some of the shifters who had transformed to gain more leverage.

One woman I noticed had come to a halt, sitting and crying on a pillar. She was stuck in the middle, afraid to move. Others were yelling at her to jump into the net and move out of the way. My heart went out to her. I stopped to yell some directions at her. If she would go backwards and to her left. She could do it. Her head looked up at me as I encouraged her onto a new path. She stood, and leapt back. Then once more, I could see her confidence coming back. She smiled and waved. Went back a few more pillars, then started moving sideways. I turned and headed forward again myself. Noticing I was again near the rear.

I finished the pillars. Only a handful of women had fallen to the nets. My legs were tired from the jumping, but I tried to run as fast as I could anyway. The next obstacle on the list, the cliff climb. According to the table team, you would rock climb your way up the cliff then down the other side. In the cliff would be large cracks. One could use to shimmy up the rocks. Coming down would be repelling ropes.

I came around the bend and saw the cliff face. Like the last two, it went all the way into the clouds. Blinking, I could see the top. It was a good fifty feet high. I looked up and down the cliff. There were two cracks. One large at the bottom tapering to the top, the other, large at the top and tapered to a point about eight feet from the ground. At ground level, a saw a small cavern that went deep into the rock. I couldn't see any light on the other side. A couple of my table team members ware there cheering me on. Actually, it was just me and the couple. All the others including spectators were moving on to the last obstacle. I looked at the couple. "What do you think?" I yelled over to them. Pointing to the large crack.

"No, take the tunnel if you can fit." The woman yelled excitedly. "It goes all the way through, but will get tighter in the middle."

I nodded in agreement and ran to the opening. I could fit through the hole. I had been in tighter spots before, so if it did shrink like she said, I should be okay, I hoped. Pearl on the other hand, would not fit, but because she was an illusion, she would not matter. I could only guess how my illusion would look diving into a to small hole. It made me giggle.

I got on all fours and began crawling as fast as I could through the tunnel. It was pitch dark. I couldn't see my hands in front of my face. I kept moving. Following the edges my body was up against. I could feel the ceiling coming down on me, and before I knew it. I was on my stomach using my elbows to pull me along. If I were claustrophobic I would be in trouble.

I had been moving forward for some time. Then I heard something. It was the sound of a soft howl. I hoped I would not run into any creatures. I wouldn't be able to defend myself or retreat. Let alone, see. The sound was growing louder. Then I felt the soft brush of fur. I stopped. Scared to do anything. Steeling my nerves for the worse, "Hello, is someone here?" I said. My voice shaky. My nerves on edge. The howl grew quiet.

"I...I...I'm to scared....I can't move." A timid voice said. I reached out, and could feel the soft fur.

"Is this you I am touching?" I asked hoping it was.

"Yyyesss." She stumbled over the words.

"OK." I took a deep breath and let out my anxiety. "I can help you. Can you trust me?"

"I don't know. I can't see, I can't move, I think I am stuck." She began to cry.

"It's okay. You only feel stuck. We are at the lowest part of the tunnel." I said, hoping I was right. If not, we were both going to be stuck. I reached out and put my hand on her fur. "Can you shift back?"

"I don't know." She said. I needed to distract her. Get her stop thinking of her fear. I inhaled another breath of air.

"I need you to listen to me. Close your eyes. Imagine the sun. Are you doing that?"

"I can't" she whined.

"You can. Close your eyes. Are they closed?"

"Yes."

"Now tell me about the happiest memory of your life." I needed her to visualize. Tap past the fear. Everything I tried up to this point was not working. In a last ditch effort, I hoped this would work. "Go on, tell me."

She began tentatively telling me about her mother. I continued to ask her questions. Reminding her to keep her eyes closed. Asking her to describe everything. Her voice was becoming less shaky. Her sentences less broken. I could no longer hear her hiccups and whimpers. As she relaxed I began giving soft directions. Transform. She did. Move forward. As she talked on about her mother, she was able to move forward. Together we worked our way through the tunnel. Soon, I could see a glimmer of light up ahead. The tunnel giving way to more room. I asked her to open her eyes. As she did, a quiet gasp escaped her throat. "Thank you, I wouldn't have made it without you." She called over her shoulder. We crawled the rest of the way out of the tunnel. She gave me a hug and wished me good luck. Then looking up at the repelling ropes, we saw we were not last.

Together, we took off running. Her, faster than I. Before I knew it, she was gone. Others were now starting to catch up to me. I had one more obstacle, then the sprint to the finish. This last one was much simpler. A single rope stretched out from one cliff top to another. Then the path continued into the trees. Below, a billowing fire pit and safety net. They didn't want to hurt you, only scare you. This, like the rope swings would not give any of the shifters an advantage. I could make up ground. Living in the fortress and around the arena for so long, balancing on ropes, or moving along them was easy for me. I grabbed the end and swung my feet over. Making sure my weight was on my heels as they wrapped around the rope. Then hand over hand, moved head first down the rope. I had passed my friend from the cave, and a few others along the way. My friend adjusted to mimic my movements, and she was moving along quickly now. A few more, muscles tired and fatigued from use, dropped to the net below. I made it across the line, dropped to my feet and took of running. Now it was a race to the finish line. I rounded the first corner, then the second. Then, entered a fog.

The path was getting cloudy. I couldn't recall my table team mentioning any other obstacles about fog. I was tired, and my mind was having troubles focusing. My legs began burning from fatigue. My mind, began drifting. Tired, so tired. I wanted to lay down and sleep.

I hadn't realized I had slowed to a walk. Now, I was barely moving. I looked around me. I could see some of the participants laying on the ground sleeping. I wanted to lay with them. Then, sirens went off in my mind. I knew this fog. This was not good. The sleep. The fog. I had been through this looking for the children.

I cleared my head quickly. I grabbed the two women on the path next to me. I dragged them back to the edge of the fog. In again I went. Dragging anyone I found. As I reached the edge of the fog, I would yell for help. I was returning from my third trip with two more participants, when I saw Raoul was standing at the edge of the fog. Horror written on his face.

"Raoul, it's the Koboldrone. There are more. I must get them." I was tired and out of breath, the game, forgotten. Now, lives were at stake.

Raoul, shook his head, he was in shock. I grabbed his shoulders and shook him. "Raoul, Raoul! We must do something." The shaking snapped him out of his shock. He gave a great howl. "Raina, you can't go back in. You may never come out."

"I must Raoul, there are others. Please take care of them, don't let anyone else enter." Before he could grab my arm to stop me, I ran into the fog. I searched for fallen bodies. I could hear others yelling into the fog for participants. I saw my friend. She was laying near a bush. I moved toward her. As I did, she was lifted by a mechanical arm and began floating deeper into the fog. I couldn't help the scream that came out of my mouth. I ran to her. Grabbed her arms and began the tug of war with the metal object holding her. I kicked at the appendages, and pulled on my friend. Dragging her as fast as I could I headed back toward the path. I could see the blue sky ahead, and headed in that direction. As I cleared the fog, I was greeted by Leon and a pack of elders. Raoul, was running toward us.

"What is going on?" Leon demanded, staring at the girl I was dragging behind me. They all kept their distance, as we were not completely out of the fog. Raoul had made it to the group at the same time I did.

"I said, what have you done! What is going on? It's that wizard causing trouble. Why are you not affected?" I could see the confusion and struggle his mind was having. I looked to Raoul for help. Out of breath, Raoul spoke up.

"Chief Leon, Raina is not to blame, it is the Koboldrone!" He was out of breath. I looked to Raoul and asked, "How many more are in there?" I was turning to go back in.

Leon grabbed my arm and swung me around. "Are you a wizard, are you to blame." My eyes were wide. He looked at me with confusion, worry, fear, and hate all at once. Raoul came to my rescue again. "No, that is Pearl, she is a contestant. I met her once before a long time ago, enchanted her against the Koboldrone. She is the only one safe from its curse."

The answer must have satisfied him for now. He dropped my arm and turned to the others. "How many more?"

"One." I didn't hesitate and ran into the fog. I searched and searched. When I was ready to give up, I spied the moving metal arm. I followed it. It led me right to her. I dragged her out of the fog to the group. My legs tired. My lungs on fire. My head light from fighting off my own will to stop and sleep. I looked at the assembly of men. They had accounted for everyone at this point. Luckily, most the women were beginning to wake. Gathering together in a frightened huddle. Leon was angry. "Why is the game still on? It needs to be ended." The others looked at him.

"Leon, it is not your decision to make." An elderly man said.

"We should end this. Begin again another time. We need to account for our people." He was pleading with the elderly man and running his hands thru his hair as he paced.

"No!" A woman yelled back. I turned to see my friend, awake. "If everyone is out, we will finish this race and be done. I would not put anyone through this again." Other participants had made there way over. We were all there. Now as a group, they were agreeing with my friend. "Yeah, and what let those that dropped out get to compete again. That's not fair!" Another participant echoed.

Leon shook his head. "Raoul, your call." Raoul assessed each participant giving an all clear to each. When he got to me, he checked me over like the others, then whispered to me. "Thank you." The elderly man from earlier lined us up and then started us off again. The race was on, now a sprint to the finish.

I tried my best to keep up with the group. They were faster in there shifted forms. I rounded a corner less than a half mile to the finish. There waiting for me was my friend. She ran pace with me. She smiled. "You have saved me twice." She started out. "So, I am returning the favor to you. I will give you a minute head start to beat me. Considering the numbers, if you do, you will be the last one to move on to round two. However, I won't just hand it to you. You must beat me there." I drew my eyebrows in, confused by this gesture. Then she started counting, "One, two, three..."

She was serious. I ran as fast as I could. Her voice softening in the distance between us. Faster, faster, I told myself. She would be on me soon. I could see the finish line. Hear the cheers. My team, Sanna, and Ethan edging me on. Sanna yelled, "Run, she is gaining on you." I didn't think I had anymore strength in me. I could see Leon at the finish line. I knew I had to beat her.

Koboldrone
Leon

I didn't know what to think yesterday. When Raoul sounded the alarm call, panic rang through us all. No one knew what to expect. When we saw Raoul surrounded by what I thought was dead participants laying at his feet. I too, felt the panic. We ran toward him when I heard the scream. I took off with a few others toward the fog filled forrest, following the sound. One of my men took a few steps into the fog. He fell down, dead? I covered my mouth, reached in and pulled him out. His breathing was shallow. He was alive. I ordered everyone to stay out of the fog till we could get some answers.

Then, I saw movement ahead. Coming out of the fog, the oversized women from some land far west. Anger hit me all at once. She must be working for the wizard. I should have insisted the games were closed. She was dragging something behind her. As she came closer out of the mist it was another participant behind her. I watched as she ventured closer to us. I began yelling at her, accusing her. If it hadn't been for Raoul, I would have had her imprisoned. That wizard, where was she?

If she was supposed to be helpful and kind. Why was she not helping?

The more I thought about it, I realized I hadn't seen her since that morning by the meadow. It is to be hoped that she was gone. Maybe she was trapped in the Koboldrone. I wondered if she had called upon the Koboldrone to attack. She could still have a part in this. I erased her and it from my mind for now.

The women insisted to finish the obstacle. Who was I to tell them otherwise. I insisted we do another roll call, accounting for all visitors and villagers. No one was missing. I didn't ask about the wizard. No one mentioned otherwise. I had my men take those that could not, or did not want to continue to the healing center. I went to the finish line, ready to instruct those that continued to visit the center when they were done. I watched as Pearl was the last to qualify for the second round. I wasn't sure how I felt about it. I left and went to the healing center to check on all the participants that had been taken there.

The girls were all doing better. After my return from the Koboldrone, we had found someone that gave us an antidote for the sleeping dead. I had seen Raoul use it yesterday in the field. Some that had still not awaken and were brought here. Now, everyone had awoken and word spread quickly as to what had happened. Odd, there was no mention that Pearl had pulled them out. Pearl, wasn't correcting the story. I found it odd and intriguing. There was something about that women I couldn't figure out. Something didn't fit.

The next game would not be late this evening. I among others had volunteered to watch over the contestants. Make sure no harm would come to them. By draw of the hat, I pulled Pearl's name. It was going to be a quick night no doubt. It was sheer luck she made it past round one, barely outrunning one of the other contestants, and beating them by a nose. If more of the contestants had awaken the day before, she may not have made it. Tonight, luck would not help her. This was a skills test. Stealth, light footing, agility. These were the traits needed to endure the longest. No one would make it through the night. I was grateful I had Pearl, she should be out first. Lace said she would keep me company, I was looking forward to time with her.

I headed to the council chambers next. Even with the festivities work needed to get done. As I walked into through the great wooden doors, I saw Sanna and Ethan talking with Raoul. They were huddled over some papers. I headed toward them. Ethan saw me first. They stopped talking and stared at me.

"Crazy event yesterday, don't you say?" Ethan commented while Sanna tucked the papers into her bag.

"Yeah, crazy. What are you guys doing here?"

"Nothing, just collecting somethings from Raoul." Sanna answered and together they all began walking toward the doors.

"Wait, you don't have to leave so soon." I called out to them.

"Yeah, we have things to do. See you later brother." Sanna called back over her shoulder.

Strange. My sister and Ethan had become distant to me after the war. Then so did I. I spent my time with Lace rather than with Sanna. Once this was all over, and Lace was my betrothed, then maybe we could work on everyone getting along. Sanna made it clear she did not like Lace.

Raoul had gone into the chamber room. Everyone was there. We looked at the map of where the Koboldrone was now infesting our lands. We were contemplating what to do. None of our talismans or potions were working to rid us of the Koboldrone. Raoul had sent word to a friend on the West coast for help. We were awaiting a response. We wagered back and forth why it was here. How it had come, and above all, what else we could do about it. Nothing was resolved. Guards were placed around the fog to stop anyone from accidentally going into the fog and being lost. For now it was all we could do. The day was nearly over. A runner came in with a note for Raoul.

He read it quietly then put it in the pocket of his robe. We all looked to him for an explanation. He looked at us thoughtfully. "That was a response from my friend. She says there is a way to get the Koboldrone to leave our lands." We all stood waiting for the answer. Raoul, stood stroking his chin, thinking. It was as if he wasn't sure about the solution. Finally someone asked, "And what is it."

Raoul responded thoughtfully. "I must talk to Raina. She is the only one able to repel this curse for us. She will decide if it is worth the risk." All of us stood in silence, looking from one to another. Baffled. What risk? Why does she get to decide? I was about to ask my questions, when Gregory did for me.

"Raoul, what is the risk for her?" He asked somberly.

I wasn't sure why he was worried about her. Obviously if she could repel it, then there was only risk for us if she did not.

"Death" Raoul responded close to a whisper. I wondered if she would do it. She owed us nothing. My heart sank. She would not help. No one would risk their life for people they did not know. I looked to Raoul, we had to ask. "Send for her." I commanded.

I waited in the chamber for the wizard to arrive. The elders had prepared the anti chamber to contain her magic. She would not be able to use it here. This was for everyone's protection. We all, especially me, had our doubts about trusting her. It was close to an hour before Raoul returned, and with him, the wizard. She was young. I was always surprised when I saw her. How someone with so much magic could be so young. She stepped to the center podium facing the panel of elders.

"I understand you have a request to ask of me." She said with a polite, confident, strength.

"Yes," Gregory began. His face took on a somber and sad expression. "We need your help. It has come to our attention that you may be able to repel the curse that has infected our lands."

She looked at the panel and stopped at Raoul. Her eyes questioning him in silence. "Tell me, where this knowledge was received." She asked, not taking her eyes off Raoul.

It was his turn to answer her, "Robyn."

"I see. Did she instruct you on how this is to happen?" She asked without hesitation.

Raoul pulled out the paper from his pocket and began to read. I watched her as she looked on at Raoul.

'If she enters the Koboldrone and allows the mechanics to take her. They will then drain her of blood. Her blood being of magic inheritance will cause the Koboldrone to react violently. It will leave your land to claim another.'

She stood unmoving. Her face unreadable. I looked at Raoul, a tear ran down his face. He did not try to hide it. "You don't have to do this." He said, emotion coming through. "She says you may not survive the drain, and if you do, you would be to weak to get out before the implosion. We will find another way. They are seeking another way."

She looked at him, then the others. Her gaze fell on me. "What would you wish me to do?" She looked straight at me. I felt her gaze hit my soul. For the first time, I felt the burden it was to be her. She wanted to know what we wished. Her gaze told me she would do what we asked. I could feel the lump in my throat. I didn't know if I could ask this girl to give her life for our safety. The guards would work. I ran my hand through my hair. I heard Gregory talk first.

"Raina, no, we can deal with this. This is to much to ask of anyone." Everyone was in agreement. Raina was still looking at me. She put up a hand and silenced the group.

"Would doing this protect the land, the people?"

"Yes." Gregory said and before he could say anything more she asked another question.

"Would it return, or get bigger if this is not done?"

We were all silent. We didn't know the answer. She was still looking at me. I shook my head, I didn't know what to say. I looked toward Raoul. She followed my gaze to him. Raoul cleared his throat. "Raina, if nothing is done, your grandfather says it can grow in size. Consume this part of the land. If you choose to do this. It will not return to this place again. Robyn can teach you how to defer it to a sealed location where it will no longer do any harm. She is on her way now. Should be here within the hour."

Raina nodded her head. She turned back to me. "This is your wish then." It was more a statement than a question. I nodded as I said yes. The elders were quiet. None saying a word. Raoul was slumped over in his seat. Tears evident on his face. I felt the guilt of asking this request. I knew if she would agree it must be done. I was thankful for her generosity. Looking at her now, I may have been to harsh in my opinions toward her. I watched as she turned to Raoul. She walked over to him, placing a hand on his shoulder whispered into his ear. He nodded in return, then left through the side door. She then went to Gregory. His face still in shock. He reached out and embraced her. Again she said something only to him. He gave a brave smile. She backed away and headed toward the large wooden doors. She looked back only once. Catching my eyes. She smiled, it was sad and brave all at once. Then out the door she went.

I looked to Gregory. He looked back at me. "She will meet us at the edge of the fog in an hours time." He stood and exited the chamber. I sat in my chair. I didn't know what I was feeling, but an overwhelming sensation came over me. I felt as if I had lost my father all over again. Why I had this feeling, I didn't know. I barely knew this girl. It was an unfortunate situation, but it shouldn't have invoked these kinds of feeling from me. I stood and decided I had to see Sanna. She liked this girl and I wanted her to hear it from me. As my sister, I owed her that much.

Sanna was sitting on the porch. Sully and drawn in. I knew she had heard. She wouldn't look at me. I sat next to her and put my arm around her. She leaned her head on my shoulder. "She's been thru so much, now this. Why does it have to end like this?" I didn't know what to say. I just held her to me. She cried in my arms. We sat there for some time. Ethan came out. His eyes red and emotional. We looked at each other. "It's time for her to go." He stated.

Sanna stood and went into the house. I followed behind her. Coming out of Sasha's room was Raina.

Surprise written on my face. I hadn't realized she was staying here. Her scent surrounding me. It was so familiar, tranquil, hopeful. My prejudice gone I could appreciate her unique scent, her soft looks, and sweet smile as she looked at me. Her scent reminded me of Lace. They were so similar. Only Lace's was barely noticeable. Raina, was pure summer and hope. This is what we needed, hope. It was befitting. I watched as she hugged my family, then she walked to me. Nodding her head, said goodbye. She walked out the door, with another women much older. I assumed it was Robyn.

We walked behind them to the fog. She gave Robyn a hug and then looked back at me. A look of for-longing, regret, and love reached me. I felt my heart ache. I didn't understand why. I had no attachment to her. She walked into the fog and we watched as she disappeared. We sat in silence for hours. Robyn being held by Raoul. I got the sense they were than friends. I sat alone. Lace sent me word she didn't want to come. She seemed almost happy to have Raina leaving. Then again, my emotions were in an upheaval for some strange reason. I was probably projecting my own relief onto Lace. Still, it would have been comforting to have her here with me.

We continued to sit. Night was falling. Then, we heard a gut wrenching scream coming from the fog. Sanna jumped to her feet and ran to the fog. Ethan and I went after her. She couldn't go in, not now. The screams continued. They went on for over an hour. Sanna screamed back. Fighting Ethan trying to break loose. Robyn had been screaming also. Her hands on her ears, screaming for it to stop. Raoul was rocking her back and forth. I didn't know how to help. I felt compelled to go to Raina, save her. This wasn't right. I couldn't recall ever feeling this strongly toward anyone. Not even Lace. The screams stopped. My mind panicked. I immediately transformed and without thinking ran into the fog.

I could feel the pull of the sleep calling to me. Wanting me to close my eyes. Rest, relax. My fear for Raina was stronger. I paused to listen to the woods and fog. Where was she? Sleep was pulling at me. I could hear Sanna and the others calling for me to return. I looked around. I could smell fire. I ran toward the smell. The closer I got to the fire, the tireder I became. Then I picked up a hint of her scent. I concentrated on that. My adrenaline flowing, I ran toward the faint smell.

The fire and smoke was getting denser. I was having troubles seeing and breathing. Soon, I came across a decaying old stone building. I placed a hand on the soot covered wall in front of me and began following it around. A feeling of déjà vu took me over. I was looking for a set of doors. A dream I had done this before. I envisioned I was following a girl. Watched her be strapped to a table. Running, running from the explosion. Her scent was strong. My daydream broke. I saw Raina crawling on the ground only feet from the wall in front of me. The fire nipping at her heels. Covered in blood from head to toe. Cuts encasing her entire body. I scooped her up into my arms.

I ran. I ran with her in my arms as the fire raged. Explosion after explosion echoing behind me. I could see the setting sun ahead. The colors vibrant. I ran to them. A final explosion sounded and the fog around me was sucked into a vacuum void. I fell to the ground. She tumbled out of my arms. She was laying on the ground unmoving. I again had that feeling of loss. I yelled for help. Desperate for anyone to come. I didn't know how to help her.

Sanna was first to arrive. The others couldn't keep up with her. She came to a running halt. Kneeling over her checked her vitals. I watched as desperation took over my sister. Ethan and Raoul arrived. Ethan picked her up and hurried to Robyn who was still some distance away. Raoul came to me side, checking me over. Gave me a whiff of the curse repellant solution. I could feel the tiredness leave my mind. Robyn was now over her. Potions, spells, and enchantments ready. All were being performed. I stayed back. I didn't want to interfere. I didn't know why I had done what I did. I felt better knowing she was out. Now, I hoped she would live.

I moved over to Sanna. She was shaking. I wrapped my arms around and embracing her. Together we found comfort. I heard Robyn stop. We both looked over at Raina laying on the ground, blood pooling beneath her body. Robyn turned. "She is still alive, but badly hurt. I hope she will live." Robyn whispered. Relief at those words filled me with joy. Sanna ran to her side. Ethan picked her up and together they took her to Sanna's. I moved over to Robyn and Raoul. They were talking.

"She may not wake up." Robyn was saying. "I don't know if this is better than being dead."

"Will you tell the others?" Raoul asked.

"No, I can't take away their hope." She said with a hitch in her voice.

"She has come back from worse. We must have faith she will come back from this as well." Raoul encouraged. He looked up at me then. Then taking Robyn by the shoulder followed some distance behind Ethan and Sanna.

I didn't know what to do. I was exhausted by the emotions of the evening. I still had the second round of games to officiate tonight. I would talk with Gregory. See if he could take my spot watching Pearl. I thought of Raina. To think, other than the Council, no one would know what had happened this evening. This girl was braver than I gave her credit for.

I went to Gregory's to ask him the favor. He inquired what had happened. "So, you ran after that girl." He smiled and punched me in the arm. "Yeah pretty stupid." I laughed. "Not the first time you've done something stupid over a girl."

I had been a young boy since I had done something this stupid. I couldn't even remember the details it had been that long ago. Gregory agreed to the trade. I told him I would stop by around three in the morning. If Pearl was still at it, switch up. For now, I needed to get some food and rest.

Awaken
Raina

I opened my eyes. Unsure of where I was at. Sitting by my side, Sanna and Ethan. She had her eyes closed resting her head on Ethan's chest. I could hear Robyn and Raoul in the distance. I looked around. I was in Sasha's room. I was alive. Joy filled my heart. I was afraid I would never see them again. See the kids. See my grandfather. I needed to protect them. Hopefully, it worked and the Koboldrone was gone for good. No longer able to haunt any other villages or my loved ones.

I tried to move, but could not. I could feel a heavy weight on my body. I lifted my head and could see an ora of magic blanketed over me. My clothing was shredded. My arms and legs still had blood seeping out of my wounds. I could feel the magic tingling on my skin. I hoped it was working. I hoped it would heal me this time. I laid my head back down on the pillow and let the magic heal my wounds. I slept for another hour.

When I awoke this time Sanna was talking to Robyn in the other room. I looked around and could see I was alone. I lifted my head. It was easier this time. Looking over my body, I could see my wounds had stopped bleeding and were sealing shut. I would definitely have more scars. I tried to move. The magical blanket that held me gave way, disappearing into the air. I sat up in bed. I was stiff, wounded and soar all over. My clothes a massive mess. I went to my bag and pulled out a fresh set. I could barely lift my arms. Moving about caused more pain and blood. I was finally dressed. My body scared with holes, claw marks, and deep cuts. Yeah, this would take a while to heal. I tried some magic. Still nothing. I tried my mirage. It came slowly, but was there. I ventured the few steps to the sitting room. Everyone turned at my arrival. Cheers, tears and attention all on me. I felt my cheeks blush. Sanna and Robyn ran to my side. Helped me sit in a chair.

"You okay. Your alive! Your awake! What can I get you? Water? Food? Do you need anything?" Sanna rattled it off so fast. I figured I wouldn't get a word in edgewise. Ethan stepped in then. "Drink. You'll feel better."

"I already feel better. I am not dead." I said with a weak smile. Sanna shook her head. "To soon for jokes?" I smiled again.

"Yes. You really scared us."

"I scared myself."

"What happened?"

"I ... Maybe another time. I ..." Emotions were taking hold of me.

"It's okay, we are just glad you are still with us. It was touch and go there for a while." Robyn chimed in.

I looked around. "Leon, ...is he here?" I asked no one special.

"No." Sanna looked around at the others, as if afraid to tell me the rest.

"Please tell me." I pleaded with them.

"Round two is tonight. He is officiating." Ethan said.

"Oh." A smile lit my face.

"No, you cannot go. You just died." Sanna said throwing her hands up in the air as she stood.

"But, I'm okay now."

"You can barely walk."

"What is the game tonight, maybe I can do it?"

It was Ethan who jumped in over Sanna, "NO! Tonight is the Ankylynx Challenge. You are in no way ready."

"What is the Ankylynx Challenge?"

Raoul now spoke. "You must fight a caged animal and survive till morning."

"And if I do, I move on." I asked hopeful. I had survived the torture of the Koboldrone. I have been in worse shape and put into worse places. I could do this. "Tell me about this creature."

Ethan just shook his head. "You are as stubborn as my wife."

"I thought I had missed it all. So, this is fate. I am meant to fix my mistake. Tell me about the creature. Help me beat this." I looked to Ethan for help.

"I think she should try." Robyn spoke for the first time since coddling me into the sitting room. Everyone looked at Robyn. Awe at her comments.

"She doesn't have to last the night. Just outlast most the group." Raoul chimed in.

"Fine, I will tell you of the creature."

So Ethan did. Everything he knew of the creature. It's weak points. It's hunting style. The works. I smiled at him. I stood to get ready. My body still ached with pain at every move. Mentally, I was ready, and that was all that mattered. I walked toward Sasha's room as I did, put my mirage back into place.

Ankylynx
Leon

I had slept later than I wanted. Tossing and turning all evening. I kept dreaming of Raina. I dreamt of her at the Arena in Nezra's Fortress. A nightmare as I watched her fend off a snapper. I dreamt of her being bound by the Koboldrone. Then being attacked by an Asbjorn. I couldn't shake the dreams. Every time I closed my eyes, it was of her. I knew they weren't true, it was just my past reinventing itself with her in it. The urge to rescue her today was playing tricks on my mind. I had to keep reminding myself they were just dreams.

I looked at my clock. It was well after three. I had told Gregory I would be there before now. Chances were, he was probably home in bed. Pearl should have rung out hours ago. I dressed and headed to the cages.

As I came around the bend, I passed empty cage after empty cage. At the end of the row, I saw Gregory. He was still here. Probably couldn't sleep. I sat next to him. "Can't sleep?" I asked. He looked at me. Tired eyes and a yawn. "Now that you're here to watch, I can." I looked from him to cage. There in the middle laying on the ground was Pearl. "You've got to be kidding me! I thought she would have rung out by now." I was shocked for a second time today.

"You and me both." He yawned again and began to stand. "She has worn out her companion. The Ankylynx is there." Pointing to a boulder some paces away from her, curled into a ball. "It fell asleep some time ago. Unfortunately so did she." He pointed at Pearl now. "Depending on who wakes up first, she will either beat that thing, or you will need to rescue her."

"Seems I've been rescuing women all day." I joked with him. He gave me a half laugh. Then slowly began walking to his home.

I sat on the boulder watching her as she slept. I heard another pair of footsteps coming up the path. It was Ethan. He paused in front of Pearl's cage. I saw her stir. She came slowly to the fencing. Moving as though in her body was stiff and unmovable. It looked uncomfortable. They exchanged a mumbled words. Ethan handed her a mug. She drank it down. He said something more to her. Then she moved back slowly, gently, to her spot facing the creature. Ethan watched for a moment then went back the way he came.

The thought of Raina entered my mind. I should ask him about her. How she was fairing? She was in bad shape. From the exchange between Robyn and Raoul, I wondered if she was still alive. Given my duties, I thought now would not be a good time to ask. He looked as if he had a lot on his mind. I watched Pearl lie on the ground. She didn't move. I couldn't tell if she was awake or asleep. An hour passed. Only a few more till sunrise. I wished I could tell her to ring out. The others had already done so. That would be against the rules, I didn't want to disqualify her when she had come so far. She was obviously a lucky person to make it this far.

I sat on my perch, my mind drifting to unimportant nonsense. A breeze began to blow my direction. I could smell Raina's scent. I looked around for her. I knew she wasn't there. I looked back at Pearl. Still lying on the ground. Funny how all these women smelled so similar it played tricks on my mind. Maybe that was my problem. They were so close in scent that it was messing with my emotions and dreams. I looked over at the Ankylynx. It was beginning to stir. I stood up. If Pearl were asleep, this would be trouble. I needed to be ready to act.

The cat stretched its legs. Then surveyed the area. It's glowing eyes fixated on Pearl. She didn't move. The ankylynx jumped down the back side of the boulder it was resting on. It prowled through the tall grass making its way closer to Pearl. I took a step toward the cage. Pearl's head moved. She was following the cat's movements. I was watching her watch the cat. As the cat got closer. I could see her begin to adjust her position. She started cooing a soft song. The cat's ears perked up.

He was listening to her. Ethan must have coached her. He helped tend the animals from time to time. It was a trick to get them to relax. Allow the workers to do their job of feeding or cleaning. It worked most the time. All the caretakers were trained to defeat the cat if needed, however. She began moving now. Still cooing her song. The cat walked to her. Arching its back and brushing her leg as she stood. She reached over and rubbed the cat's back. He nestled into a ball at her feet. She continued to stroke its head and back. I could swear I heard the cat purr its pleasure. She tamed this unpredictable wild creature into a house pet. It seemed no more harmless than a young pup.

For the next hour she sang her song and stroked the cat. It soon rolled away and strolled back to its cave. She laid down on the ground and continued to sing. Soon, the singing stopped. She moved to the fence line and called for Ethan. It looked like something was wrong. She was holding her stomach. I could see something dark seeping through her clothes.

I walked down the hill, and stood at the fence. I was trying to assess the situation. She looked up at me. Her face was warn and tired. She looked to be in pain. I looked her over from head to toe. On the fabric of her shirt a black stain was spreading over her stomach and sides. I touched her thru the fence. She flinched. It was damp. As I brought it up to my face to see in the moonlight. It was blood.

"What happened? Did it attack you?" I was trying to wrap my mind around it. I hadn't seen anything. Nothing to worn me of this type of injury. The cat gave no sign it was attacking her. She caught her breath. "No, I'm fine. The cat didn't hurt me. This is from something else."

"What else? Why are you here if you were injured?" What did she have to prove? I entered the cage and stood facing the fence to talk with her.

"You wouldn't understand. I have to do this. Have to try." She was pleading with me. "You must leave. I need to stay. I can't ring out."

"You must and are. I am calling it." I didn't feel bad. I knew she was last. Chances were she would move on. I doubted she would be disqualified for not staying the entire time. I looked at her. The sun now coming up behind her. I smiled. "Looks like you don't have to." She turned to see the first ray of light break the horizon. She smiled back at me. I called for help. Not realizing I was waking the cat at the same time.

I heard the screech. Before I could turn around, Pearl pushed me to the side. She ducked under the leaping cat. It missed us both. Quick thinking on her part. She was on her knees. I could see she was in pain. She was watching the cat. It was preparing to pounce. It leapt at her head. She tucked and rolled out of the way. I was on my feet now between her and the cat. Her hand touched my back.

"I got this, get to safety please." She said with surety. I was again shocked by this women. Before I could give it any more thought, the cat pounced at me. I threw a blow and knocked it down to the ground. The cat shook off the hit and was circling us. I could hear the running of footsteps. It was a matter of time before others would be here. Pearl was on her feet. Her breathing was labored. I could hear the hitch in each breath. The cat was getting ready to strike again.

It jumped toward pearl this time. She was quick on her feet. Moving out of it's way and catching it by the tail. She gave it a quick pull then swinging it with both hands, throwing it toward the cave. It landed on its back with a loud thud. It took a minute to get back up. Conceding defeat, retreated back into its cave. I looked at Pearl, the sun now well over the horizon. She had blood dripping from her midsection. It reminded me of Raina. I scooped her up and headed out of the cage.

Ethan was first to arrive. One look and he snatched her from my arms and took off running, I assumed to the healing center. The others came around the corner.

Commotion and questions attacked me. I explained she had other injuries. The caretaker's face went ash white. These cat's are blood thirsty. They can smell blood a half mile away. Will come in swarms to get to a bleeding prey. She was lucky that cat didn't kill her. As much blood as I saw, that cat should have been on her all night. I began wondering how she managed thru the night, and how she got those injuries.

I turned in her time. I had to put the time I entered the cage. Even though she did make it through the challenge. She hadn't needed my help. There was something familiar about the way she moved. Protected herself, and tried to protect me. I had seen it before. I just couldn't think of where. I stopped at the elders chambers. I wanted to see the results before heading home and getting some rest before the next challenge started. I ran into Raoul on my way in.

"Hey, are the results ready?" I asked. He seemed a bit pre occupied. He was deep in thought. When he looked at me, I knew he hadn't heard a word I said.

"Leon!" He sounded surprised to see me. "Is it over?"

"Is what over?" Now I was confused, where we talking about the same thing, or was he asking me something else.

"The Ankylynx Challenge. Is it over?" He asked again, more edginess than before.

"Yes, just finished. I was hoping I could see if Pearl made it. She was a trooper till I saw her bleeding. I wanted to make sure I didn't get her disqualified or cut." I explained.

Raoul's eyes grew wide. "Bleeding? She's bleeding again?" He didn't wait for me to answer, instead took off running out the building. I didn't know what was going on. The healers would assist her. She would be fine with a little healing lotion whatever it was. I headed into the chamber hall. There on the table was the list. Pearl had made it. I wanted to tell her the good news. Odd. Again, I wanted to be at her side, in her presence. I had only felt that way around Lace and then felt it earlier after the fog around Raina. I knew my emotions were messed up. I decided after I gave Pearl the good news I would seek a healer to get my emotions checked and back on track.

At the healing center, Pearl was not there. They had no knowledge of any injuries she may have received or how she would have received them. They did mention Raoul had been in collecting some supplies. I asked for something to mend my emotions. Without explaining to much, I didn't need gossip spreading the village. I was denied any solutions. They directed me to see Raoul.

He may know how to help me I was told. I wasn't sure what to do. I needed my emotions back in check. I also hadn't confided in Raoul in years. We had grown apart after his betrayal of the council. I pondered my dilemma. I decided it could wait. A good sleep would probably do the trick.

I reached my home and crawled into bed. Again I was wrestling with my dreams. Only this time it was Pearl plaguing my mind. I was going to have to talk to Raoul.

Sleep
Raina

Last night was hard. I had always been taught that pain, illness, even ability was all in your head. If you thought you were sick, you would get sick. If you thought you couldn't do something, then chances are you couldn't. My mom had instilled in me positive thinking. Going to round two I needed to be positive in my abilities and healing. I didn't think of the pain. I didn't think of my tiredness. I had walked days with broken bones. Had been sliced open by various weaponry and animals. To succumb to my injuries would be a mistake I would pay for with my life. I needed to prove to myself that I was going to be all right. I still had such strong guilt over Leon's memories, I had no choice in my mind but to go to round two.

Ethan had brought me straight home. Robyn had performed her potions and magic to work at healing my body. The activeness of the cat was no help to my healing. If it wasn't for Ethan's tranquility song, I would be in worse shape. I was still laying on Sasha's bed. My bleeding had stopped and scabs were beginning to form for a second time. Robyn said she was trying something more powerful, now that my body was letting the magic help heal me. I had tried some magic last night. A protection wall between me and the cat. Nothing. I was still only privy to my parlor trick. Worse of all, I couldn't disguise my smell completely anymore. I smelled less of burnt cookies and more like me, according to Sanna and Ethan. Both were happy to have the burnt smell gone.

The next round was two days away. Ethan said I had made the cut. I was happy for the small break. It would give me time to heal. I spent most my time sleeping. Rest seemed to heal me the best. Robyn and the others would take turns visiting and checking on me. Raoul even came once. He was conducting business with Sanna and Ethan. I couldn't hear much. It was something about Erebos, a drink, another contract. I reminded myself to ask when the morning came. I drifted into unconsciousness.

I slept for a full day. It was late evening. I could barely feel the blanket of magic. I lifted my shirt and looked at my scars. They were completely scabbed over. As long as I didn't make sudden moves, I would not bleed again. My stomach growled at me. I frowned at the sound. I slowly sat up in bed and then tried to stand. My mind began to spin and I lost my balance. I could feel myself falling. Two hands grabbed me around the waist, catching my fall. My eyes were dotted with colors. When I was able to focus and see again, I looked up at Leon.

I could feel my cheeks blush. What was he doing here? Sanna was right behind him. I looked to her for sympathy and help. He set me down on the bed but kept his hands on my shoulders, holding me steady. I closed my eyes and let my head stop spinning. I looked to Sanna again for support.

"I asked Leon to come by." Sanna stated. I looked from her to him. He was to close. He had squatted down to eye level. I was staring into his golden brown eyes. "Are you feeling better?" Leon asked.

"Yes, I think my head is done spinning. I should be okay now. I would like to try standing again." I went to push off the bed but was met with his strength pushing me down.

"Nope, you need to sit here a few minutes before trying that again." He was looking at me. I watched his eyes move to the old scars and cuts on my arms. He turned one of my arms to look at the brands still printed underneath. He then let his eyes drift down to my legs. More scars, cuts and bruising. He let his hands trail down my legs. Then stopped and lifted my foot. He looked closer and then traced the almost invisible scar that ran under my ankle in a half circle. I had done that our first night together. He looked up at me. I could see the sympathy and sorrow in his eyes. "What has happened to you?" He asked sincerely.

"Life, it's not always peaceful." I didn't know what else to say. I couldn't risk telling him about us. I couldn't bare the hatred he had for me at one time to come back. I gave him a shy smile. He returned mine with a sad one of his own. "Please sit here for a while. I will bring you what you need." He patted my knee and stood up.

"Thank you, I could use some water and something to eat." My stomach growled in agreement. I saw his lips lift at the sound of the growl. He left for the kitchen. Sanna stood in the door way. I waved her over.

"Did you find out something, is that why he is here?" I felt both embarrassed and hopeful. Could this be the turning point for us?

"We did, but that's not why he's here. I received word our mother is on her way. She will be here in a day or so. Wants to interview the nominee's." She paused. She looked like she was deciding what I could handle to hear. Then with a flutter of her eyes, decided against it.

"Okay, so it looks like there is more you want to say. So tell me." I looked at her with my serious face.

"Later." She looked out the door into the other room. I knew what she meant. Leon. I had to wait for him to leave. She held my hand. "Are you okay?"

"I feel much better. A good nap did the trick." I said yawning.

"You were asleep for a full day and a half." Sanna laughed

"What? No! Oh, no! Did I miss the next game?" I was appalled no one had woken me. Our plan! Everything!

"No, its tomorrow." She laughed.

I let out a sigh of relief. Leon had entered the room. "What is tomorrow?" He asked.

"The last game to decide who is our nominee." Sanna said sarcastically.

"Are you a fan?" Leon asked to me.

"Yes." I didn't dare expand. If I was telling the truth then I absolutely was a fan of me.

"Are you cheering for anyone in particular?" He continued.

I looked to Sanna for help. She just smiled, waiting for my answer.

"I am cheering on Pearl." I took the sandwich off the plate he held and took a big bite. I hoped it would end the conversation. Sanna gave a soft chuckle.

"Leon, maybe we should let her rest. I don't want to excite her while she is healing." Sanna said as she stood and began pushing him out the door.

Leon looked over his sister at me, "I'm glad to see you are doing well." Then he was out of the room and out the front door. I put my hands over my face. Aauugghhh. I took a smaller bite this time of the sandwich. I could feel the nausea seeping in. I was done eating. I set the sandwich to the side and leaned back on the bed. Sanna came in.

"Sorry, I had to tell him about mom. I thought he would be gone before you woke. I was extremely worried, you had slipped into a coma. You had been out for so long."

"Sanna, breathe. I'm all right. I just overdid it yesterday, or the other day. I am feeling much better."

"So," her eyebrows raised, "it's the first time he's been interested in your well being. That's a good sign." She smirked as she said it and gently hit my thigh.

I blushed again. "Maybe it's a new beginning for us." I sighed, the thought bringing me peace. It was so hard not to put my arms around his neck when he was so close. I wanted that again.

Sanna squeezed my knee and stood again. "Get some rest Raina, tomorrow will be another busy day for you. You will need your strength."

"Do you know what I have to do tomorrow?" I asked.

"No, but I have Ethan asking around to find out. We want to make sure your prepared." She walked out of the room shutting the door behind her. I swung my legs over the edge of the bed and went back to sleep. I heard Robyn come in some time later and begin her potions and chants. The heavy blanket back over me, giving me peace.

Confused
Leon

I had to leave Sanna's or else I would have made a big mistake. It started the moment I entered her home. I could smell the sweet aroma of summer. It was pure and intoxicating. I found myself craving the scent. It was strong, and came from Sasha's room.

"Sanna, who is here?" I had to ask, I no longer trusted my senses. Given I had associated this smell with three women now, Raina, Pearl, and Lace. My mind was confused.

"Hush, you'll wake her. It's Raina. She needs her rest. She has much to recover from." Sanna said pulling me into the kitchen to talk. From there I could barely see the fragile form on the bed. I felt that strong urge to go to her side. I shook it off. Sanna began talking about mom. Something about her coming, I wasn't sure. My mind was distracted and I couldn't stop looking toward the room. Sanna hit me a few times to get my attention.

"Yeah, yeah. Mom coming got it." I was looking back at the room again. "Sanna, do you know where Ethan took Pearl? I wanted to look in on her. Make sure she is okay?" I turned from the room and looked at my sister.

She fumbled the mug she was holding and it landed with a crash. Shattering the clay in pieces on the floor. She grabbed a towel and I came around the island to help her. "Grab me another towel will you." She ordered. I did as she said. She was finishing cleaning when I asked again, "Do you know how she is?"

"Who?" she played dumb.

"Pearl? Where is she staying?" I had asked around town and no one knew where she was. They only knew Ethan and Sanna had been rallying around her.

"She'll be fine. Ethan took care of her. She is fine." Then she changed the subject on me. "So are you picking up mom or will I?"

"What, oh, mom." I was distracted again. My gaze back on the bedroom. I saw Raina stir.

"I can get her. She will stay with me while you have Raina. What time?" I didn't hear what she said. I was watching Raina move to a seated position. She looked fragile and pale. Her back were I could see it was covered in scars, scabs and bruises. It looked like she had been through an explosion. I hadn't realized it, but I had been walking toward her. I stopped at the door frame. I could hear Sanna telling me to come back. Raina was working on standing.

I could hear my brain yell at her to sit back down. She wasn't ready. I took a giant stride and stretched out my hands in time for her to fall into them. Saving her from a hard crash to the floor. She was dizzy and from the look on her face, I could see she was unable to focus. I held her for a minute. It felt familiar. That feeling of déjà vu came over me again. She lifted her head and smiled at me. It was a beautiful smile. I wanted nothing more than to hold her. I shook the feeling off of me and set her down on the bed. She tried again to stand up. I forced her down again.

I looked her up and down. Then slowly I looked over the markings, scars and scabs on her arms. Then down on her legs. One faint scar caught my attention. I felt I had seen it before. An image of a swollen ankle, dirty sock and bloody dagger entered my mind. I shook it out. It didn't make sense. I had not met this girl prior to the war. I certainly hadn't seen her since. I was confused. My mind playing tricks, taking images from Lace and my past and inserting her. "What has happened to you?" I asked in my head. When she answered, I realized I had said it out loud.

I looked up at her. My heart full of sympathy and sadness for all she must have gone through. I wanted to be able to fix it for her. I knew I shouldn't, or couldn't. Our faces were less than a foot away. My senses were being overrun by her scent. My hands burning from the touch of her skin. In that moment I wanted nothing more than to lean in and kiss the girl. I needed a distraction. I asked what she needed. Gave me an excuse to leave the room. Distance myself from her.

Sanna and Raina were talking when I came back. It was about the games. I had forgotten all about them from the moment I entered Sanna's house. I would be betrothed at the end of them. My heart sank a bit. I inquired if she was a fan, who she was cheering for. Anything to not think about kissing her.

She was cheering for Pearl. Figures. Everything had to be so complex. What had started out so simple, me wanting to marry Lace, was now getting complicated. I found myself cheering for Pearl and wanting Raina. Sanna was pushing me out the door. I was glad to go. I needed to get away from them both. I told myself when Lace starts competing it would be different. That's the only reason I cheered for Pearl now. It was the absence of Lace.

The final game for the village nominee was tomorrow. Chances were, it would not be Pearl.

Round Three
Raina

Today was the last event. Round three. The winner of this single event would be the nominee. No pressure. Hah! It was a simple game of hide and seek. They would hide an object. We were to seek it out. First to find it and turn it in wins. I was anxious for the game to begin.

We, Sanna, Ethan, and I as Pearl, headed to the ceremonial ground arena. It was the place of the final game. It had been transformed from the open aired finish line some nights ago to an enclosed monumental domed building. As we walked inside the domed shape arena there were two sets of doors. One marked participants the other spectators. They wished me luck, then moved through the doors and up a series of stairs. I took a deep breath. The butterflies in my stomach were sewing knots. I was anxious, nervous and excited all at once. I scratched my arm. The two days of rest and the magic Robyn had performed had done enough to seal all my wounds. They no longer bleed or tore when I moved. Now they itched. I tried not to scratch the delicate scabs off my body. I reached out and opened the set of doors. It took me to a second set of doors larger than the first.

Upon my approach, they opened automatically. I stepped forward into a perfectly white room. It was small in size, but the grandeur of the height made it feel enormous. The other nine women were there. I was the last to arrive. We still had plenty of time before we started. My nerves were growing in anxiety. I looked around and noticed some white benches on the wall. I took a seat in one. The other women were conversing. I could only catch glimpses of the conversations they were having in hush tones. Something about why I was here. I didn't give it any thought. The women that were left had all been belittling me from day one. I didn't expect their opinions had changed much. I closed my eyes and thought of my family. Trying hard to block out the chatter and anxiety.

It wasn't long till the rear set of doors opened. Together we walked out into the arena. Above us were rows of seats. I looked around for Sanna. Instead I was greeted by the Elders, Leon, and other nominees seated high above the ground in a special section. They were framed by beautiful white flowers and ivy. I looked over the crowd, finally spotting my friends. They were seated together at the far end from where I was. I could see Sanna biting her nails in anticipation. I felt my stomach flip in my own anxiety. I looked about the arena. There was a white glistening curtain hanging from below the seating separating us from the rest of the arena. I could not see through the white of the curtain. Reaching above the curtain and spread throughout the building from floor to ceiling were beautiful carved white columns. They were wrapped in the white flowers and ivy. The room looked as if it was plucked from the clouds. It gave me a sense of calm and peace. I was happy for the change in my demeanor.

An Elder announced the welcome. He stood on a platform that elevated him down to ground level from the other Elders seating. With a loud voice he announced we would begin. The crowd cheered. I could see my little group waving banners with my name. It made me smile. I hoped I would do them proud.

We stood before the Elder. He handed us each a small white jeweled box. It was intimately crafted with images of the flower surrounding us, the diamond jewels at their centers, glistening in the light. We were asked to open the box. I gently lifted the lid. It was empty inside. I looked around to the other contestants. They were looking at something. Sniffing it, holding it. I only saw air. Then it hit me. It was an enchantment. You saw an enchanted image, not the actual item.

Great! I had lost the ability to switch between real and magic. Now, I couldn't see the magic. I had no idea what I was looking for. Panic filled my mind. There was nothing I could do but watch in agony as others looked for my unknown item. I looked at Sanna. She read my face and horror crossed over hers. I shrugged my shoulders and smiled. Defeated before we even started.

The boxes were returned. A chime rang out and the curtain separating us lifted. I stood looking at piles and piles of items. There were mountains of jewels, and mountains of gold, and mountains of diamonds. Every type of treasure was here. I watched as the other women ran to various piles sniffing and digging as though it were trash. I wanted to leave. Disappear. I had no where to go. I looked around the room. The women completely spread out.

Around the outside of the arena, guards stood in place. A smile crossed my face. These were real. Had to protect the village treasures. I found myself adoring the columns of flowers. One column especially caught my attention. It had something sparkling from behind one of the flowers. I walked toward it to get a better look. This column was farthest from the piles. It stood surrounded by five other columns at the end of the arena. As I approached the column I could see it was a delicate, beautiful pearl and diamond pendant necklace. I hoped it was not dropped from a spectator above.

It was a good ten feet off the floor. I wouldn't be able to reach it. I looked at a guard nearby.

"Would you mind giving me a lift up. I think there is something there."

I pointed to it. He looked at me, then at the adjoining two guards on either side. Both shrugged there shoulders. He looked back at me, eyes moving up and down my body. "Sorry miss, I don't think I can lift you."

I wanted to laugh, if only he saw the real me. I looked to the second guard. "Will you be so kind as to help him lift me to that spot there?" I asked.

He snickered at me and gave me the same look over as the other. "Fine" he grunted out.

I walked with them over to the column. Placing my feet in each of their hands, waited for them to lift. Up I was going. "She's lighter than she looks" I heard one say to the other. "Good thing" the other responded. I was almost there. It was higher than I thought. I pushed up on my toes to get the few inches I needed. Then with a flick of my finger, it came loose and fell to the floor. I watched it roll a few paces away. I began to waiver in my spot, the men holding me were watching the necklace roll and forgot they were holding me.

With a clear of my throat to get their attention, they brought me to the ground. I let go of my helpers and turned to get the necklace. Standing over it was a short black haired woman. She picked up the necklace.

"Drop this?" She said with an unpleasant smile.

She took a whiff of the necklace. "Lucky me." She snapped out, and ran to the podium where the elder stood.

I looked at the guards who were just as shocked as I was. The announcement was made. The object had been found. We had a winner. My heart sank. It was over. I stood unmoving. I could hear the crowd cheering. I walked along the wall of the arena to the now open doors. I headed to Sanna's. It was time for me to go home.

Adjustment
Leon

I was in shock when they announced the winner as Aida. I had been watching Pearl. I could have sworn I'd seen her grab the jewel first. Somehow Aida had it. Turned it in. I felt so disappointed it wasn't Pearl. I should have felt relief, but I did not. I waited till everyone had left before leaving my seat. Lace wanted to get ready for tonights celebration. So I was alone, or; alone as one could be with guards and the other elders.

I got up to go. I could hear a discussion at the ground of the arena. There voices drifting up to me. I boarded the platform and sent it to the ground. Elder Marshall was talking with two of the guards. I stepped into the conversation.

"It appears we may have a problem with our winner." Elder Marshall commented. I looked from him to the guards. They grunted there respects to me.

"What is the problem?" I asked.

"They say another contestant found the object and dropped it. Aida picked it up and did not return it. Instead, turned it in." He was very skeptical. "The rules are whoever finds it and turns it in is the chosen winner. They claim she only did half."

"Is this true? Are there any other witnesses?" I asked.

"There is a couple who have stated the same story. I am doubtful to believe them." He continued. The guards were standing vigilant trying to not interfere as we talked.

"Are they not credible witnesses?" If there were four individuals that saw this, then chances were it was true I thought.

"Not in my opinion! None of these stories are credible. Regardless she would be disqualified. She had help. That is against the rules. " He was admit in his statement. A closed case.

"Why is it up for discussion then?" I asked the guards.

"You see," the guard started then stopped abruptly as he received a glare from Marshall.

"Marshall, let him speak. I want the entire story." I turned to the guard. "Continue" I ordered.

"She was to short. She couldn't reach the object she had found. She asked me to lift her up so she could reach it; and I did. Well, we did. She looked to heavy for me, so she asked him as well, and so we did. We lifted her up and she got the necklace out of the flower. It fell out of her hands on the way down. Aida came over to watch her. When it fell, Aida picked it up. She smelled the object then said it was hers and took it."

"So, no one showed the contestant where it was?" I asked.

"No sir. She pointed it out to us. I still didn't see what it was until it hit the floor." One guard responded.

I looked to Marshall, "Sounds like she didn't have help. The rules allow them to use anything in the arena to get the object. These guards would be no different from any other tool." I waved my hand toward them.

Marshall looked at me. "There is no way she could have found that item unless she was told where to look."

"What do the other witnesses say?" I asked Marshall. He turned to one of the guards talking with us and sent him to fetch the couple. I watched him leave. When he came back he was with Sanna and Ethan. I shook my head. I should have known.

"Don't tell me, you know she didn't cheat." I said shaking my head and running my hand through my hair.

"You know she didn't Leon. You know I don't lie. This is wrong and you know it." Sanna screamed out.

"Let me guess, the woman is Pearl?" I was exasperated. Why did it have to be her? Now I was in a fix. Did I side with Marshall even though I thought he was wrong? End my problems with these women confusing me, or side with the others and fight for Pearl to move on. I was torn inside.

I looked at Marshall, "This is a matter we must decide as a council." I wanted the pressure off of me. My emotions were already torn. It was cowardly on my part to put the decision to a vote. From the look Sanna was giving me, she knew it too.

I sent word to the other members to meet at the arena. The arena was cleared. We were alone. Guards were gone. Sanna had left. The discussion of this problem began. Both sides were heard. Why she should move on, why she should not. I opted to abstain from my vote, claiming it would not be ethical for me to persuade or deny a potential mate. The Council men agreed. I gave a soft sigh of relief. The debate was ended with Raoul's proposal. Allow both women to move forward. The next challenges would prove their worthiness. The board voted and Pearl was allowed to move on with Aida. Raoul volunteered to let her know.

The meeting ended, I left the arena with the others. The dance was to be at the edge of the market place like before. I needed time to get ready, and clear my head before seeing these women. I also needed to check on Raina. I had been thinking about her all day. I had hoped to see her in the crowd, but, she was not there.

While waiting for the game to start, I had thought about leaving and spending the afternoon by her side, keeping her company. Then the doors opened and Pearl along with the others entered the arena. I forgot about Raina and began watching Pearl. There mannerisms were so similar. Her scent, reaching me from that far away. I couldn't help but stay. Now, all I wanted was a break.

I could see my home. As I rounded the side, Lace was waiting for me on the porch. I gave her a half hearted smile. So much for a break from the women I thought to myself. She was dressed to kill. Looking fabulous in her long silky red strapless gown. She was twirling her pendant that she always wore. Ever since I had met her, she wore it. Never took it off. Said it was special. It was pretty enough. I walked up to the door to let myself in.

"What no kiss hello?" She asked in a sultry voice. She closed the distance between us. Wrapped her hands around my neck and leaned in for a kiss. I gave her a short soft peck. She pulled back and pouted her lips. "That's not a kiss." She leaned in again and kissed me harder. I wanted to be alone. So I gave in to get rid of her. "So we haven't talked in days and I missed you." Lace pouted out. She followed me into the house. Took a seat by the fireplace.

"Sorry, I've been a bit busy." I confessed.

"I found a pre-party we could go to. So get ready and we'll head out." She batted her eyes at me.

"I don't have time for that now, Lace. I have things to do. Sanna wanted to talk to me, I've been putting that off for a day. I need some rest. You go without me. I will meet you at the event." I sighed.

"You never come with me anymore. How do you think it makes me look?" I could see her attempting to control her anger.

"Look, it's not that I don't want to come, but maybe I need to show an impartiality considering all things." As soon as I said it, I knew I had made a mistake.

She threw her hands in the air, and began stomping around the room. Her face was consorted, her cheeks red. Her voice went up an octave. On she went. How could I treat her this way? I didn't love her. I was making her out to be a fool. I was embarrassing her in front of her friends. I needed to get my priorities straight. It didn't end. I tried to reason with her. I had no luck. Anything I said was twisted in its meaning. Somehow adding to her anger. At this rate, I wasn't going to get any rest. I tried to be logical. This was tradition. I was bound by duty and office to the winner. She couldn't accept that. Now she was on a rampage about all she had done to get here. The challenges hadn't even started and she was already overreacting. We had never fought like this before. I frankly, didn't like this person she was being.

If I wanted to salvage any relationship with her, I would have to concede. So I did. I pulled her into my arms. She struggled to be released. I kissed her moving mouth till she stopped talking. When I thought it was safe. I ended the kiss. Still trapping her arms against my body I looked at her. "Lace, enough. You know I love you." She tried to interrupt. I kissed her again. "Lace!" I said more forceful this time. "You know the rules. Wether I like it or not. I have to be impartial."

She began pouting her lips and looked as if she was going to start the arguing all over, but changed her mind. "Lace, I want you to be happy. I want you to do your best to win." Or did I. I was feeling torn as I said the words. "Lace, go to the party. Enjoy the festivities. Enjoy your friends. I cannot go. I will see you later." I gave her one more kiss. Then released her toward the door. She hesitated for a moment. Looked down at her pendant, fidgeted with it in her hand for a moment longer, then plastered a smile on her face and left my home.

I don't know what just happened there, I was glad it was over. I was confused. Tired. I went to my room and took a nap.

I had slept later than I wanted. Sanna and Raina would have to wait another day. I needed get ready for the banquet tonight. I was already running late. I showered, changed into my black dress suit and headed for the door.

I could hear the music drift down the path before I saw the decorations and people. It was a great turnout. Adjoining villagers had come into Ladow for the announcement and final challenges. The aroma of food, made my mouth water. I looked over the crowds of people. To the right of me was Sanna, Ethan, and Pearl. I was excited to see her. I walked their direction.

Sanna saw me first. A dramatic roll of her eyes and turn of her shoulder told me she was upset for not meeting again, but forgiving. I stood next to her anyway, and in a way only a brother can, lifted her up and hugged her hard. "I'm sorry about not coming by today. What did you want to talk about?"

"Not here you oaf! You need to see me tomorrow morning it's important."

"Everything is important with you Sanna."

"No, Leon, this is important to you. Now let me go."

I put Sanna down and said my hello's to Ethan and Pearl. They were all a bit to quiet for my tastes. I looked at Sanna, "Guess I'd better take my seat at the table. Looks like they want to start off the night."

"Take Pearl with you. This is all new to her." Sanna said. I saw the brief unspoken exchange between women. "O..K." I responded. It was going to be new to all of us. We had never had four women in a challenge before. The Elders were making some last minute adjustments and changes. I didn't even know what they would be. From here on out, I would be kept out of the loop. I grabbed Pearl's hand and walked her to the banquet table. Her hand was soft and gentle. It was smaller than Lace's. Felt natural in my own. We got to the table, Lace was already there waiting in the seat closest to mine. She saw Pearl's hand in mine. I could see the instant jealousy and anger rush to her face. I could already tell, this was going to be a long night.

Announcement
Raina

My chair was at the last one at the large rectangular table. At the far end was Raoul, then a series of Elders, then Leon, Lace, Teela (the Elders nominee), Aida, and then finally me. The only advantage of being at the end was I didn't have to talk to anyone. I preferred this solitude. That and the fact that I was first to be served. The food looked so tasty and smelled heavenly. I tried everything that crossed my plate. The table in front of me gave me some odd looks and snickers, but I didn't let it bother me or suppress my appetite.

Once the food was cleared, Raoul welcomed and announced the finalists. Each of us getting cheers. My fan base had grown. It made me smile. With the announcements behind us, the dancing began. I sat in my chair as instructed earlier. Leon was to dance with each of us. We were only to dance with him. I was okay with that. I heard the others mumble in jealousy, but truth be told, one night of dancing wouldn't matter in the long run.

I waited patiently for my turn. He danced with Lace, than Teela. Then Lace again, she was overly protective.

He than asked Aida, but was interrupted by Teela. I watched as the fight to get his attention continued. The night was half over and the three ladies couldn't make it thru a hole dance without one of them cutting in on the other. It was somewhat comical. I was glad we hadn't danced. I would be so nervous in his arms. I wasn't any good at dancing. The only time I had danced had been with him and Raoul. I remembered Leon showing me how, not judging me. I wanted that again, but I wanted it in privacy. Not a speculation for the village to see, or to be interrupted by one of the other women. Nope, sitting here was good.

The night was winding down. Still, no Leon. He was dancing with Lace again. The others were standing off to the side seething with jealousy. Probably plotting their next move. I decided to take the opportunity to find Sanna and say goodnight. Tomorrow was another busy day. I wanted to be ready.

I cut through the crowd of dancing couples, then over to the far side of the festival. In the trees surrounding the market, I was able to move about unnoticed, looking for my friends. I stopped by a tree and leaned against it. I was debating to keep looking or head out. I closed my eyes for a minute, the nostalgia of the dance touching my emotions. A hand touched my shoulder. I looked up and saw a young brunette gentleman. He smiled.

"You already done with the festivities?"

"Yeah, I was thinking of heading home now."

"Oh, that's to bad. I was hoping to talk with you, ask you to dance. I'm a big fan of yours."

"Ah, thank you, I think. I appreciate the offer to dance, but can't. You know the rules being a finalist." He looked disappointed. "Tell you what. If I get out, the first dance is all yours. Deal."

"Deal." He bowed slightly and headed back into the crowd. It was sweet. I looked back over the dancing couples. Still no sign of Sanna or Ethan. I turned down the path to head home, the music slowly fading in the background.

"Leaving so soon?" A deep voice said from the shadows of the trees around me. I stopped in my tracks. Leon came out from the brush. He stood next to me. He looked very handsome in his black dress robe. I felt my cheeks flush. I watched as he brushed off some leaves and twigs still stuck to his clothes.

"Hiding" I answered back as I threw my hand on my hip, and cocked my head.

"Can't one venture thru the brush without hiding?"

"One I guess could, but given your entourage I doubt one would be alone in the brush."

"Okay you caught me, but if you tell anyone, I will deny it. You never did answer my question. Are you leaving already?"

"Well, yes, and as such, I bid you good night."

"Wait a moment. I am required to dance with all the participants. As you did not take your turn." He bowed slightly and extended his hand to me. "May I have this dance?"

"I don't know how to really. You see I've only danced a few times, and I wasn't very good then. Maybe another time." I said as I looked down at the ground embarrassed. He stepped toward me. Then took my hand in his and lifted it to his lips. He set a light kiss on the top of my hand.

"I am bound by duty to dance with you, but I would be honored if you would accept a dance with me."

I stood thinking. I would love to be held in his arms. Memories of our last dance came flooding back. I also didn't think it was a good idea. Before I could respond his arm wrapped around my waist and he pulled me closer. I was facing his chest. He swayed me to and fro. I tried watching my feet. As to not step on his. He removed his arm from around my waist and lift my chin up to his face. Then his arm encircled me again. I watched him watching me. I could see his own battle waging behind his eyes. I had some hope his memories were returning. I stumbled again. He responded by pulling me closer.

Now our bodies were melted into one. I laid my head on his chest. At some point, without me noticing, I was stroking his neck and playing with his hair. It all felt so right. I didn't want the song to end. It did. When it did, he stepped back a half step. Enough to put space between us. My embarrassment came flooding back. What was I thinking stroking his neck, laying on his chest? He probably thought me a love sick school girl. Which I was, but that wasn't the point.

He looked at me again with those confused eyes. Then before I could react, leaned in and kissed me. It was soft at first. He tasted like honey. Sweet and tender. Then he stepped into the kiss. It began to grow deeper, lustful. I couldn't help my own response. I tangled my arms around his neck and let my hands twist in his hair. I was lost in the moment with him. It was all so magical, till I heard in the distance the call of Leon's name. I willed it to go away. Again, I heard the echo in the distance. He heard it that time to. The kiss ended. He looked at me with confusion. Then I saw the emotionless mask that covered his face. It was our first dance all over again. Every emotion of rejection I had then came flooding back ten fold. He turned on his heels and headed toward the soft female voice that was calling his name. I watched until he left my view. My hands shaking and tears now streaming down my face, I turned and ran home.

Morning came. Sanna was at my bedside encouraging me to get out of bed. The first challenge would be starting in less than an hour. Sanna looked at my puffy eyes and blotched cheeks.

"What happened last night? And don't tell me nothing. I saw you head into the woods. I saw Leon exit the woods angry. So, what happened?"

"He kissed me. Or, he kissed Pearl."

"What!!" "You have to start at the beginning."

"I had started heading home, and he came out of the brush. He asked me to dance."

"Well, did you."

"I tried."

"Then what?"

"We danced. At the end of the song he kissed me."

"What did he say?"

"Nothing. Someone was looking for him. He ended the kiss and took off."

"Nothing. That idiot! Men! Why is he fighting it?"

"Sanna, it wasn't me, it was Pearl. He may not even like me."

"Nonsense! You are one and the same."

"But were not. I don't look anything like Pearl."

"You see, that's the point. You are as daft as he is sometimes."

"Really Sanna."

"Really, if he likes pearl with all her flaws and imperfections, then he'll like you. All the others are cookie cutter shaped women. It's a flaw us shifters have."

"Sanna, that's not true."

"Oh, but it is. Have you ever seen a shifter that doesn't have long flowing legs?"

"No, but.."

"Have you ever seen a shifter that was not fit and sleek?"

"Well, no, but I haven't been out there looking either."

"So you see, your competition is three of the same women. You my spunky friend are different, that's what makes you intriguing."

"I don't believe your logic, but I will agree to get you off my back."

"Best thing you've said all morning, now get ready, we have a man to rescue."

I got up, got ready. My mind drifted back to Sanna's words. Why was Leon angry? Was it me, or something else. Was she really right about him liking something different? I was certainly that. I heard the front door open and a mumbled set of voices. I stepped out of the bedroom. Leon was there. He turned and looked at me. I realized I had not put up my appearance of Pearl.

"Raina? I thought you were someone...." He trailed off in his surprise.

"Good morning Leon."

"I forgot, how are you feeling?"

"Fine thank you."

"You're moving about okay?"

I realized he was looking at the bruises and scabs on my arms and legs. My cheeks flushed in embarrassment.

"Yes, I am doing fine. Only visible damage. Nothing more."

His face saddened a bit. He turned to look at Sanna.

"What did you want to talk about?"

Sanna looked at me. We had decided she would talk to him without my presence. We didn't want to upset him to much. I took the cue.

"Leon it was pleasant seeing you." On that note I headed out the front door. I stood on the porch for a few moments, checking for any prying eyes. Then with a silent spell, I blinked Pearl into place. I began the slow scenic walk to the arena alone.

Contract
Leon

"You want me to believe that I knew her, and that I had my memories wiped."

"Yes, I have proof!"

"Why would someone do that? I knew we couldn't trust her. I shouldn't have saved her."

A slap stung the cheek of my skin. I looked at Sanna. Anger seething below the surface.

"Yes, you should have. If you read the darn contract you made, and the one Erebos switched out you would see your error."

"But you don't have them?"

"No, I said, Erebos destroyed your contract. Go talk to him. He'll tell you what it said. What you wrote."

"Why would I trust that babbling lunatic? Ever since the war he has been nothing but insane."

"Because he regrets his actions and will tell you the truth. He is the one that did this to you both."

"Even if he did. Why would she take away memories? That makes no sense."

"She was hurt and felt betrayed. Can you blame her."

"Yes, that's the point!"

"Forgive her, talk to her. You'll see that you love her."

"Oh, so now I love her. It's not just that the contracts were switched or that I was given some kind of potion to hide the truth. I loved her now also. That is outright ridiculous."

"It's not. You went to rescue her from the fortress. You wanted to forge the allegiance with a marriage proposal. You."

"If she did this, then why not just give me back these so called missing memories of mine and it will all be cleared up."

"I told you she can't. Something happened in the war and she doesn't possess those abilities anymore."

"I find it all convenient. I knew she would cause trouble. Here it is. Some made up story to stop me from happiness."

"Is that what you think? She doesn't want you to be happy, I don't want you to be happy."

"I don't know what you want from me lately. You have been distant and cold. You won't even talk to Lace. We only talk sporadically at best and of things of no consequence."

"You did that when you began listening to that harlot. Not me."

"Don't call Lace a harlot. You don't even know her."

"I think I do. Better than you anyway."

"You may not have a choice. She will be my bride."

"Will she, and what if she doesn't win? Then what little brother?"

"Look Sanna, there is no conspiracy that took place. I don't love Raina. I certainly would know if she took my memories. Erebos cannot be trusted. We are done here. I need to get to the arena."

"Fine, but you do yourself no favors in not talking with him, or with the other members of the old council."

I was done arguing with my sister. I needed to clear my head. It had begun throbbing five minutes after we started the argument. I also needed to get to the arena. Lace would have my head if I didn't go and support her. She was still mad at me for disappearing last night at the celebration.

The women were so competitive. Lace was over protective. I didn't have a chance to get to know any of them. It was frustrating and flattering at the same time. I had been hidden in the trees for some time when I smelt Lace coming. As I looked out, it was Pearl. I was pleasantly surprised. I had forgotten that they smelled the same. Then again this morning at Sanna's, I smelled Pearl, and it was Raina. I would need to talk with Raoul about this. In fact, maybe Raoul could shed some light on what Sanna was arguing about.

He could talk with her and set her straight. I would need to ask him to do that today. The quicker I straightened her out, the faster I could concentrate and enjoy the next few days. I ran to the arena. The event was about to start.

I got to my seat high above the beams and rafters laid out below. There were levels upon levels of thin beams. Mazes of dead ends, twists, turns, vertical and angled ramps. The goal, get to the other end without falling off. First three on to the platform, move on. A safety net stood a healthy ten feet from the ground. Ready to catch any who fell.

The Duggars, a small animal made with interlocking spines and fur, the shape of a round ball. It had taloned feet, and a sharp beak. They would be dropped onto the beams when the bell rang. They were fast. The spines in their fur covered with poisonous slime. If spiked by one, your muscles would be paralyzed for hours. We had healers on hand to deliver an antidote potion to those stung. You not only had to navigate the beams, but you had to avoid the Duggers.

I looked around the arena. The women were lined up on there prospected colored platforms. The bell rang. The Duggars were dropped. I watched as the woman ran toward the Duggars.

I looked around the room. Raoul was here. He was sitting a couple sections over, I weaved my way over to him. He caught my eye and waved me to sit.

"How are you fairing Leon?"

"I could be better."

"Yes, when one is hunted, it can be tiring."

"It's not the women. Well, I do have some questions about that too, but right now, I need to ask you a favor about Sanna."

"I am here to help Leon. Shall we go somewhere more private to talk?"

"Yes, that would be a good idea."

He followed me up the stairs and into one of the council chambers glass box seating. It would be private here, no gossips or spies to worry about. From the glass, I could still keep an eye on Lace in the competition.

"Please tell me how I can help?" Raoul asked as he sat next to me.

"Sanna. She has this crazy conspiracy theory about the council and me, I was hoping you could talk with her and straighten her out. Let her know she is putting her faith in the wrong person. You know, let it go."

"What is this theory of hers?"

"She claims, Erebos tricked me. Used a potion on me. I in turn had my memories stolen from me because of it."

"How did Erebos trick you?"

"Sanna believes I loved Raina. I wrote an allegiance contract for her. I would know if I did I would think. If I recall, we did ask her to sign a contract. It was fair to both sides. She refused."

"You have gone back and looked at these contracts."

"No, Sanna says they were destroyed. I find it all convenient. She has a soft spot for Raina and is trying to push her feelings onto me. I just need her to hear from someone she trusts that she is wrong."

"Did you request an audience with the old members of the council to discuss these claims?"

"No, I don't see the point. If she had proof, then I would investigate. Without it, it's just a far fetched story. Would you talk with her?"

"I will, let me ask you. Does Sanna normally lie or tell far fetched as you say, stories to you?"

"No. She's never done this before in her life."

"Now you think she is?"

"I don't think she is, I think she's confused. Has her stories mixed up."

"Who is she getting her story from?"

"Erebos of all people."

"Oh, I see. And he is not to be trusted?"

"He's crazy. Everything out of his mouth is nonsense."

"So why do you think Sanna would seek him out?"

"I don't know, I'm sure she had a good reason."

"Yet, you don't believe her."

"If I believe her, than what. I stop the challenges. End my relationship with Lace. All for what, a memory of a love of a person I don't know and can't remember. As chief, that is not the wise decision. Who's to say I would love her now. Things have changed."

"What if your memories return to you one day. Will you regret not getting to know her again."

"I can't think like that. If I looked back on what I know now would I have done some of the things I did. No, but I have learned from them. I can't stop my life now for a maybe."

"I guess you are correct in that. So it is best you not consider any alternatives to the path you are on."

"When you put it that way, it makes me sound like a stubborn fool."

"I do not mean to insult you."

"No, you didn't. I will talk with some of the others if you would please talk to Sanna."

"And what of Raina?"

"I can't talk to her. If she did take my memories away, how do you forgive someone for that."

"That is a choice you have to make. If you find what Sanna says to be true, then maybe you can see why Raina would do what she did."

"I doubt that. Whatever the truth is, it's in the past. Down there, that is my future."

Raoul stood and left the box. I sat there thinking about his questions. I looked down at the field of play. I could see Pearl comfortably moving across the beams. Jumping down a level, then pulling herself back up. Her moves reminded me of someone. I had seen them before. I couldn't place it. My head began hurting again. I looked for Lace. She was moving the wrong direction. A heard of Duggers on her trail. I made up my mind, after the event was over I would look into Sanna's claim. Raoul had a point. She has never lied. Most trustful person I know, so if she trusted in Erebos, then there was a good reason. I should at least believe her, regardless of how far fetched her claim was.

Duggers
Raina

I was making good time. The beams were similar in size to that of the fortress. I was at home on them you could say. The wood had a slight bounce to them. I could use this to my advantage when jumping from one to another. I had perfected the technique of balancing and moving when I was very young. The heights didn't bother me. The narrowness was nothing new to me. Honestly, I felt at home and at ease on the beams.

I stopped for a moment. Listening to the tapping of the Duggars, and looking around to strategize my moves. Teela was in front of me. She moved swiftly shifting back and forth from wolf to human form. Lace and Aida were behind me. Aida was moving back to the safety of the starting platform. Lace, was about to be cornered if she wasn't careful. I could see the path I needed to take. Below me, I could hear the clucking of the Duggers. Behind me a glance back told me they were making there way up a ramp and would be on my beam in no time. I took off running. I would need to leap across the open section between beams. If my luck held out, the Duggers wouldn't continue up the ramp to the upper beam and cut me off.

I held my breath as I leapt. It was a bit farther than I anticipated. My back foot slipped off and I fell to my knees on the beam. I held the sides with both hands, getting my balance back. I could hear the clucking behind me. They were on the beam I had just left. I needed to pull myself up a beam and head to my right. Then I could cross down on a ramp and continue to the platform. I hurried myself to the crossbeam and jumped high reaching for the beam. My fingers barely curling around the edge. I had a good grip. I used it to hoist myself onto the beam. I no sooner got up and on my feet when I could hear the Duggers closing in behind me. They took the ramp and were gaining fast. I would have to drop down an extra level to avoid them. I ran to the end of the beam then letting myself slide on my backside, flew down the ramp onto the lower beam. The Duggers were hot on my trail. Rolling down the ramp at faster speeds than I did. I needed to get off this beam. I tried a sideways jump to the parallel beam. Missed. I could feel myself falling. I stretched out my arms and with a painful bang, caught myself with one arm on the lowest beam.

I could feel my arm dislocated from my shoulder. I needed to stay in the game. If I fell, the game was over. I would be the fist one out. I swung and turned my body so my other arm could grab the beam. I pushed up, trying to keep the pressure off my dislocated shoulder. The pain was immense. I needed to pop it back in to eliminate some of the pain and be able to use it again. I looked behind me. There was a vertical beam. If I ran my shoulder into the beam, maybe it would knock it back in place. I turned on toes and ran shoulder first into the beam. A loud pop echoed in the arena. I felt the bone shift into the socket. I wanted to let out a scream of pain, but held my tongue.

No sooner did I get my shoulder into place, I could hear the tapping of claws on wood, and the clucking of the Duggers. I looked behind me and saw them coming down a beam.

I jumped trying to grab the beam above me. I missed. I ran further, grabbed hold of the vertical beam and wrapped my legs around it. I began pushing myself up the vertical beam to the rafter above. I could hear the Duggers jumping and snapping there beaks below me. I reached the top of the rafter and hoisted myself back up. I took a moment to look around.

Lace was trapped hanging from a vertical beam. She had Duggers on both sides of the lower beam and Duggers on top. She wasn't going anywhere without being stung by their fur. Aida was prancing along the start line. Looking for a way to get around the Duggers that had trapped her. They were following her every move. I looked for Teela and saw her just in time as she crossed the finish line and the crowd burst into cheer. I looked back at the others. I saw the determination on there faces. They were going to make a run for it. Stings and all.

I turned and ran as fast as I could to the finish line. I could hear the Duggers behind me. I could see Lace, or I think it was Lace in wolf form, gaining on me from the side. Then I heard the scream. I stumbled from the distraction. Gathering my balance with ease, I didn't look back. I kept running. Jumping from beam to beam. I heard the ring of the bell. The contest was over. I slowed to stop. I could see Lace and Teela at the finish line. I looked behind me. Aida was no where in site. Down below, I could hear the argument taking place between Aida and a grounds keeper. She had fallen. The contest was over.

I was relieved to move on. Then I heard the clucking. I looked back to see a hoard of Duggers racing toward me. I took off running again to the finish line. With a dive onto the platform, I barely escaped the sting of the Duggers.

I laid on the platform for some time. Shoulder aching. The others just scoffed at me. Lace asked for assistance. I could see her one leg was paralyzed. She had taken a few hits from the Duggers. Their spikes sticking out of her leg.

A healer worked his way up the ladder and administered the antidote potion. After a few moments she was moving her leg around. Then stood. She then continued down the ladder. I could hear her asking Leon to assist her home. I rolled to the edge and watched as he put his arm around her and escorted her out of the building. I laid back down on the platform, the healer now hovering over my body.

"That was some fall you took. Held my breath for you. Can I check your shoulder?"

"Yeah, I dislocated it, but I think I popped it back in."

"I saw. Must have hurt."

"Sure does."

"We were all pulling for you."

"We?"

"Yeah, the other workers and me."

"Thank you. That's very kind."

"Well, you inspire us. You're not like the others."

"Inspire. I don't know about that. You don't even know me."

"You aren't selfish like they are. They only want to win. You, to us anyway, you seem to care about people. Look at the games. You helped all those people in the obstacle course. And I don't just mean from the Koboldrone. We watched you encourage others. Help them out."

"Well, it was the right thing to do."

"Then, in the cage, you were kind to the animal. The others weren't. Shows you respected them."

"I'm sure the others would have been kinder to if they knew the song. I feel I had an advantage there."

"Yeah, but they did know the song."

"Still, I have done mean and bad things to in my life. If you knew me, you would not think so highly of me."

"I think we would. You remind most of us of the girl wizard, Raina."

"Is that a good thing?"

"Yeah, most of us, me included, were saved by her. She also helped numerous village members escape torture and death from the fortress. Granted, no one is facing death, but you remind us of her. We were a bit sad to hear she was here in the village but not competing."

"So you wanted her to compete?"

"Yeah, but you're the next best thing. No offense!"

"None taken."

"We heard she got rid of the Koboldrone for us. No one has seen her since. I hope she's okay."

"I know she is."

"Do you know her?"

"Yeah, I do."

"Oh, would you tell her thank you from us all."

"I sure will."

"Now how does your shoulder feel?"

"Much better thank you."

"Did you get stung by the Duggers?"

"No, I somehow managed to avoid them all."

"You were moving good out there. You know Raina would run along the rafters in the fortress."

"I did learn from her."

"You are so lucky. I would love for her to teach me."

"Maybe I can put in a good word for you."

"Would you. That would be awesome. There is a group of us that would love to learn some of her moves."

"I'm sure she would be flattered. Tell you what. She has a few hours this evening, if you want to meet her in the meadow at the South end. I'm sure she can show you a few things."

"Really. Can I bring my friends?"

"Yes, that would be fine."

"Are you sure she would be okay with this. I mean, don't you have to ask?"

"I know her so well, I know she'll say yes."

"Thanks Pearl." He took off down the ladder. A smile in his step. He practically ran to the exit with excitement.

I laid on the platform until I heard Sanna yelling for me from the ground.

"I'm coming" I yelled back.

We walked back to the house. Sanna gave me an update on Leon. They had the talk. Now it was up to him. He could accept the truth and we, that is Raina would talk with him, or he wouldn't. My nerves were eating at me. I was glad I would have the distraction in a few hours to busy my mind.

Evening came and it was time to head out. I made sure my scars were hidden. I still felt self conscious. I made it to the meadow a bit early. I wasn't sure what I was going to teach, or what they were looking for, but I would try. I sat in the middle of the meadow. Alone. My eyes closed. I tried to focus on my family back west and my mother. Nothing. I couldn't see them. I couldn't find them. My magic was so blocked it frustrated me. I closed my eyes again. This time searching for Leon. Still nothing. I heard a crack from a branch breaking. I turned in my seat to see if they had come. To my surprise, it was Leon.

"I didn't mean to disturb you." He said. "It's just that I come here when I need to think."

"I know." I said gently now feeling guilty that I had chosen here to meet my fans. "I was waiting for someone, then we will leave you to your solitude. I'm sorry I intruded." I stood and began walking to the path the others would come. He walked toward me.

"You don't have to leave."

"No, I shouldn't have suggested here. I know this is your place."

"How do you know?"

"You told me once a long time ago."

"Did we know each other well?"

"Not at the time. Our past is very complicated."

"Sanna told me some things today. I can't quite believe. She said you altered my memories. Took them away. Why would you do that to me?"

"I was hurt. It wasn't right. I am truly sorry for doing so. I hope one day you can forgive me."

"How can I forgive you? You changed my whole perception of life. How do I know what is real and what is not?"

"I can only tell you to trust your instinct. I hope you can take comfort that I only took myself out of your mind. Nothing else. If you are looking for the truth your memories should return."

"Why not just give them back to me?"

"I can't. I have lost my powers to do so."

"I don't believe that to be true."

"I would find it hard to believe also, however, it is the truth."

"Why would I trust you when you admit to what you have done?"

"You can't. I see that I have upset you. I didn't want to do that. I just wanted to set things right. I should go."

"No, you can stay. I will go. I have one more question." He paused. "What did the contract say?"

"Contract?"

"When you stood in the council before the war, there was a contract presented."

"Yes, you said you had worked it out, but the one you presented to me asked me to be your slave. Live in solitude in your cells to do the bidding of the council."

"I wrote that?"

"You told me you did. That's why I was hurt. I trusted you. I realize I was still wrong to do what I did."

"I signed this contract."

"Yes, you all did. Erebos presented it, your signature was at the top. Again, I'm sorry I reacted the way I did." I could see the denial in his eyes. "I'm sure if you looked you would find the contract. It was bound with magic. Unbreakable."

"How do you know this?"

" At the time I could see the magical fingerprint."

"And now, I guess you can't!"

"Until the Koboldrone I could. But now, I can't. I only see things as they are. I can no longer see the illusion of magic."

"Another convenience on your part."

"If you feel so. Look I can't help you with this process. You need to discover the truth for yourself. It is the only way you will know what is real as you put it. If you have any questions about our interactions. I will be here for a few days more."

"Why are you here?"

"I told you, to set things right."

"This is how, by getting Sanna to do your dirty work?"

"No, this was Sanna doing her own interrogation. She discovered the truth on her own, asked me to come back. Enlightened me on what may have happened that day. I regret what I did. I had hoped that by being here. By participating you would see me for me, and you would begin to remember and eventually forgive me. I see now, that cannot be. I will take my leave."

He let me walk away. I could feel the pain of a broken heart all over again. He wasn't going to forgive me. He absolutely wouldn't be pleased to find out I was Pearl. It would be just another deception to him.

Another reason to not trust me. I made it almost to the fork in the path when I ran into the healer and a small group of his friends.

"We are so excited to meet with you. Thank you again for working with us. It is an honor to learn from you."

I looked at this wide eyed group, so eager and excited. I needed to push my feelings aside and follow through with my promise.

"My apologies everyone. It appears the meadow is taken. I have no place for us to train."

"That's okay. They cleared out the beams and the arena is empty. The labyrinth won't go up until tomorrow morning."

"Well then, let's head over there. Now what would you all like to learn?"

The entire walk there, the crowd told me every story they heard and asked every question they could. How I got around in the fortress? How come I didn't leave earlier? What the snapper was like? Had I ever fought anything as deadly? My head was spinning by the time we got there.

We entered the arena. The floor was covered in dirt. They wanted to know how to defend themselves. I thought back to the lessons Raoul had given me in the fortress. We began with the basics. Using sticks as weapons, I taught them simple defense moves, like ducking and weaving. Looking for your opponents weak points. Discussing ways to avoid the fight. They were all good students, attentive, patient, and above all, positive. I enjoyed working with them. The night was getting late. I ended the lesson. I had requests for further lessons, but gracefully declined. I was going to head home. It was time for me to leave. My students were disappointed, but understood.

 I headed out of the arena back towards Sanna's. As I approached the house, I could hear Sanna yelling inside. There was a heated argument happening. It didn't sound like Ethan was on the other end. I didn't want to intrude. I headed back down the path to give them some privacy. I walked for hours, letting my mind wonder. Not paying attention to where I was, I found myself in the meadow again. I was alone. I sat in the field of wild flowers. My head barely higher than the stems. The moon now shinning high in the sky, so I laid down on the soft petals. Soon I was asleep.

 I woke to the feel of a touch. I was being lifted up. Panic rang thru my mind. I turned out of the arms and jumped to my feet. My hands posed for action. If only I had my daggers I thought. I let my eyes focus. It was Leon. He had taken a step backwards away from me.

"I'm sorry I scared you."

"What are you doing?" I snapped back at him.

"You looked so peaceful, I didn't want to move you, but sometimes we get beasts that come into the field. I didn't want to see you get hurt."

"I can take care of myself."

"I can see that now."

"I'm sorry, you were trying to be nice. I..I mean, I'm sorry."

"I'm the one that should be sorry."

"Thank you for waking me, I need to go." I turned from him and began running toward the path that would take me to Sanna's.

"Stop." He said.

I came to a stop and turned to look at him in the middle of the meadow. I waited for him to talk first.

"When was the first time we met?"

I stayed where I was, afraid he would bolt like a scared rabbit. Keeping my voice soft I recalled to him our first encounter. "You were in the Koboldrone building. I ran into you in one of the rooms." I held my breath waiting to see if he would respond.

"You were looking for something?"

"Yes, I was looking for my family."

"You found them I think someone small."

"Yes, I found them. You helped me carry them out of the building before it exploded and disappeared. They were much younger then."

"I think I was trying to remember. I had a dream about you and the Koboldrone. It was after you had gone in there again."

"Maybe that's what triggered the memory."

"Maybe? What happened after that?"

"You offered to let us come to Ladow on our way to the North."

"You were hurt. Your leg?"

"Yes, I had hurt my leg in the Koboldrone. I had internal bleeding and needed to cut my ankle open to let the blood out."

"I held your foot."

I chuckled it seemed funny to me that he would remember my foot. He continued talking as he ran his hand thru his hair.

"When I saw your scar at Sanna's it seemed familiar to me."

"It was one and the same."

"You can understand why this is hard for me Raina, can't you."

"Yes, I don't expect you to forgive me."

"My head hurts."

Neither of us had moved since he began asking questions. I decided to close the distance between us. "I know a trick if you like."

He looked at me with skepticism. Afraid to trust or touch me. I kept some distance between us. Scared rabbit, I reminded myself.

"If you pinch the skin between your pointer finger and thumb, then rub in small circles while keeping the pressure, it will release the tension you are feeling."

With one eye cocked he rubbed his hand gently. "It works!" He was surprised. I chuckled again.

"I know that laugh."

I sobered fast. "Is there anything else you want to know?"

"Were you at the fortress?"

"Yes." The thought brought back mixed feelings. I felt a chill run up my spine. I shivered in response.

"Are you cold?"

"No, just a memory."

"What happened there?"

I sat on the ground. This was not an easy answer. "I don't really talk about it."

"How long were you there."

"Eight months the second time."

"You were there before?"

"I was, but that can keep for another time."

"I was there eight months."

"I didn't know you were their till the escape."

"In my dream you were running, trapped in a cage. Is that true?"

Another shiver crawled on my skin. The thought of barely making it out played in my mind. I distracted my thoughts with a blade of grass. Leon came and sat by me. "Is it to much to ask."

"No, I owe it to you. I had been caught helping your floor escape. That's when you revealed your identity to me. You had been hiding in a makeshift transformed state."

"I remember that. I don't remember you."

"You were assigned a cell with Kayley. She instructed you on the rules."

"Yes, how did you know that."

"I was the one who visited the cells and brought you extra food and blankets."

"And the cage? What of that?"

"The Raiders liked to torture the prisoners by making them earn their right to live. The Snapper was apart of that. They had just killed a group of prisoners. I was locked in a cage above the arena. You were..."

"I was in a cage with levers watching."

"Yes, you were the gate keeper. It was part of the plan. When I had a chance, I broke through my cage and ran to the exit. You had to lift the gate."

"I saw the snapper attack you."

"Yes."

"You fought back. You got free somehow. Disappeared into the wall."

"Yes, than we met up and came back to Ladow."

"Why not use your magic to protect yourself, or leave the fortress earlier."

"I didn't have magic then."

"Does that have to do with the marks I saw on your arm?"

"Yes, they protect and bind me. When we figured out what they were, Raoul helped me to discover and learn how to use my magic."

"Raoul?"

"Raoul and I are old friends."

"You knew him before. You had been here before."

"Yes, and No. I had met Raoul outside your village. That's where we became friends. I had only been to Ladow with you."

"I brought you back here twice?"

"Yes."

We sat quietly next to each other for what seemed like an eternity. I felt we were making progress. I could tell he was still working things out in his mind.

"I found the contracts."

I held my breath, waiting. He ran a hand thru his hair. I could tell he was in conflict.

"I spent the afternoon talking with some of the old council members from the war. One of them had saved both contracts."

"So, it's true, there was a second one." Now it was my turn to ask questions. Everything had been speculation up to this point. Now that he confirmed it. My interest was peeked.

"Yes, I drafted the first one, and Erebos drafted the other."

"And the one I was presented was Erebos's?"

"I think so. I still don't remember. I know a contract was presented. Considering Sanna's words, it sounds like it was Erebos's."

"What did yours say?"

"It doesn't matter now. Things are different. We are different."

"What of us? Can we move past this?"

"I just don't know, I don't know if I even want to remember now. It all feels as if it is more of a dream than anything else."

"Is it because you love Lace?" I didn't want to hear the answer. I knew he confessed his love for her. Maybe that was his destiny now, where once, it could have been us.

"Maybe, I don't know. It's complicated and confusing. I have responsibilities to the village and my position. Maybe if I weren't in this process it would be different. I could get to know you, see if my memories return. For now, regardless of my instincts or how I feel, it is best for me to concentrate on what lies ahead. Be best for you to."

I didn't know what to say. I didn't know how to react. He had made up his mind. I began going over the options in my mind. Do I leave now? Do I continue in this charade as Pearl and hope for the best? Do I fight for him? He said it was complicated, if only he knew how complicated it was. I was fighting my own inner battle when he spoke again.

"I just don't know what I want anymore."

"What do you mean?"

"Here sitting with you, I think of Lace and Pearl. When I'm with Lace, I think of you and Pearl. When I'm with Pearl, I think of you. I find it emotionally draining and complicated. I know we can't have anything. I just don't know why I am at odds with myself."

"What reminds you of each of the other women?"

"It's your scents. They are the same. Sometimes just a hint off, but lately, you all are exactly the same."

"Anything else?"

"Not with Pearl and Lace. They are completely different in everything, manners, confidence, skills. Actually, I watched you at the arena today teaching for a while, and you and Pearl are very similar. I would almost bet she could mimic you to a tee."

"Is that so bad that we are so much alike?"

"No, it's not. Only, she is a possible option if she succeeds. You are not. You're not a participant, and I am bound by tradition."

"I see, and how does Lace fit into all this."

"I loved her before we started. Now I don't know. I only think about her, when I catch your scents."

"So, if she didn't smell like me, you wouldn't be as attracted to her?"

"No, she's a beautiful woman. My wolf instinct is attracted by scent. Helps you find the one you are bound to for eternity. That's what I want. I want that kind of bond, love and attraction. So if any of you didn't smell the way she did, I don't know. I don't know if it would make a difference or not."

"Okay, so smells aside. Inner wolf quiet, who would you want to spend your life with?"

"That's the complicated part. I can't separate out the scents from the feelings."

"I see."

"Even sitting here with you, I have to control my urges. They are overwhelmingly attracted to you. Your scent drives me crazy."

I was shocked at his revelation. I took a few scoots sideways to put some distance between us. He watched me and smiled. A soft chuckle left his lips. "That won't help. I could smell you on the path here. That's how I found you."

I smiled back, now blushed with embarrassment. "I can leave. I don't want to make things worse for you."

"No, you bring me peace. I may want to kiss you, but I also feel comforted and calm around you. Please stay a while longer."

I scooted back over to him feeling silly I moved in the first place. He reached for my arm and moved my sleeve up to see the bruises and scars. "I know these are not all from the Koboldrone, how did you get them?"

"Some are from my battle with Nezra. His magic was powerful, leaving marks where his curses hit me." His hands went to my other arm, lifting that sleeve also. I felt chills go up my spine. The touch of his hands on my skin bringing heat and warmth. Now I wanted him to kiss me. "Some are from my fall. I broke most of my bones, were they penetrated my skin, it left marks."

"Didn't you have healing potions."

"We did. My Aunt tried them all. Nothing worked. It took years to gain back my mobility and strength."

"Is that why no one saw you?"

"Yes." The memory of the pain was still fresh in my mind. I picked up my blade of grass again and fiddled with the ends. He lifted my chin to face him.

"I'm sorry for your pain Raina." He was so sincere. I was touched by his words. He left his hand on my chin, and giving in to temptation, leaned over and kissed me. I let it happen. I didn't fight it. I didn't want it to end. He was kissing me, not Pearl. I let myself be lost in the moment. I don't know when it stopped, but I was out of breath when we did. He looked at me, his eyes wild. His hands on my neck and back. I waited. The sun was coming over the horizon. He removed his hands from my body and stood. Then reached out to pull me up. "I don't know why I did that. I should get ready to pick up my mother. She comes in today."

"The interview"

"Yes, she interviews the participants. Can I walk you to Sanna's?"

"No thank you, I'll be okay. I should go. Leon, I am sorry I took your memories, or caused you any pain or confusion. I was just trying to protect us."

"I know. I hurt and betrayed you to. I want you to know that what ever happens, I hope we can be friends. I think I understand why you did what you did. I just can't forgive you for it."

I could feel the weight of the world on my shoulders. I also had the ache of regret. The realization that he had kissed me good-bye. I turned from him and ran to the path toward Sanna's, the sun now lighting the path.

Deception
Leon

I couldn't help myself. After sitting and talking with Raina all night, it felt so right to kiss her. When I first saw her in the meadow sleeping, I felt I was on the verge of a memory returning. That feeling of déjà vu hit me again. We had been here before. I had watched her sleep before. I felt a strong urge to pick her up and take her to my home. I needed to protect her. As I did, she awoke. She was quick and defensive. Again, I had that feeling of déjà vu. It was so familiar and yet not.

I was glad we talked. It had been a long and exhausting day. After the arena, I spent some time with Lace. She needed my attention and care. Odd, I didn't have as strong a desire to care and protect her. It entered my mind, but was easy to dismiss. When I had satisfied her needs, I went to see Erebos. He lived at the far end of the village.

"I thought you may come at some time to confront me." Erebos giggled out.

"I need answers!" I was frustrated and annoyed by his giddiness.

"And you think I will give them to you?"

"I don't see how it benefits you not to give them to me."

"I will tell you the truth, as long as you give me your word I will not be charged for my actions." Another giggle escaped his lips.

I ran my hand in my hair unsure if I could trust him. I had so many questions. He picked up on my frustration and doubt and began talking.

"Leon, I was once like you. Nigh-eve, trusting, honest, but, like you, things change." He giggled again. It unnerved me. "I met Nezra long ago. You were only a boy." He pulled his sleeve up and showed me a small brand at the bend of his wrist. Similar to those Raina had on her arm. I looked at it. Curiosity peaked. "So, I see I have your full attention now." He giggled and sent a chill down my spine.

"What is it Erebos?"

"The mark of Nezra. The promise to be ruler of this land."

Shocked and horror rushed at my emotions. Ruler? Promise? I had a feeling things were about to get more complicated.

"Go on." I insisted.

"I met a man many years ago. He promised me wealth, power, and honor." Another giggle escaped his lips. "In return I would give my loyalty to the High Wizard."

"You mean Nezra?"

"No." He giggled again. "Nezra branded me with this symbol of strength. It was then that my life began to change."

"How did it change?" I began to worry.

"You my boy." He giggled again. "I made you ruler so I could control you. I made Ladow the strong hold it is today."

I sat in shock. My mind regretting the information it was given. "My father, my mother?"

"Yes, I orchestrated the removal of them both. So I could rule. You think you could have done anything without my wisdom. I was the ruler of Ladow like I was promised. You were merely pons to use."

"You killed my father for his position?" I yelled across the room. Anger now steaming from my skin. My instincts ready to tear him apart.

Erebos giggled. "Don't be shocked. You like being Chief. You like the power as much as I do."

At that I punched Erebos in the face. No longer able to control my rage. How dare he compare me to himself. It only enraged me more.

Erebos rubbed his chin and let out a giggle. "Was working to, till that girl arrived." He looked at me then with an eerie glint in his eyes. He took a few steps away from me and sat in a wooden chair by the window. Now looking out at the dark forest beyond.

"She was a threat to my plans. I couldn't have that. She needed to be dealt with. When I found out she had magic. That just made it easier for me to betray you both. When you presented your contract of alliance, I took the opportunity to turn her against you."

"What did you do?" I said through clenched teeth.

"Nothing. She did it all. All I had to do was present an alternative. A new contract, a potion of confusion. I couldn't have ever hoped for the retaliation she did to you. It was perfect! You with no memory. Me with all the power." He sighed at the memory.

"So how did it go wrong, you are obviously not in power and will never be because of your betrayals."

Erebos pounded his fist on the chair rail. "Don't you see!" He shouted back. "I was betrayed. I was to be ruler. The war was to go around Ladow. If that tramp hadn't returned I would still be in power!"

I was shocked by the admission, and appalled by the actions of our Elder. "Where does your loyalty lie now?"

Erebos laughed again. "I will always be loyal." And he stood and gave me a majestic bow.

I growled back at his response. Gave a short whistle and waited for a guard to arrive. Erebos sat back in his chair and stared out the window. We no longer talked. Only the sound of a soft giggle penetrated the tension between us.

When the guard arrived, I explained Erebos's confession and had him escorted back to the prisons until we could put him on trial. As for now, it would have to wait till the contests were over.

I headed to Gregory's home next. I needed a familiar face and to talk out what I had just heard, about my family and Raina. Gregory had been on the council then, as well as, when I was captured and taken to the fortress, somehow, I thought maybe he could help me somehow. I wanted some clarity and confirmation from someone I trusted. I hoped I could trust him, he was a loyal advisor to my father at one time.

We talked for hours. He was just as dumbfounded about Erebos' admission as I had been. He promised he would look into the events of my father's death and investigate for a trial with the council. I felt I had made the right decision in trusting him. The conversation then changed to Raina. Gregory went to his study and found an old dusty wooden box. He pulled out a scroll wrapped in twine.

"Erebos deceived you both. I knew it when your argument changed. Then when you threw your contract in the trash I retrieved it. I knew one day, you would come asking about it."

"Why didn't you come to me sooner with this information?"

"I knew you had changed. You no longer had your memories. Instead you were mean and bitter towards anyone different. You were no longer the man I knew you to be. I also knew it wouldn't be enough to change your mind, change your feelings, change you back to who you were. You needed to do that on your own."

"Now, what do I do now? Trust a woman I don't know. Hope she isn't this all 'High Wizard' manipulating us all? I can't do that."

"Ah, that's where your wrong. You always trusted her. She, unlike Nezra or Erebos, has never given anyone a reason not to. Besides, we have never seen any other wizards besides Nezra and Raina. So where is this High Wizard? He said he met a man then said it was Nezra. It makes more sense that Nezra sent someone to recruit for him and that he is the High Wizard."

"I get what you're saying. You should have come to me. I would have changed."

"Look over the last few years, you were quick to justify your actions of hate instead of seeing Raina for her. Think about it. What did you say when I found her on the ground broken and bleeding?"

"I hoped she was dead." A sick feeling entered my body. I was disgusted with myself for the hateful things I thought of her and said to others. She had only helped us. The wall she made, the fight with Nezra, the protection of our elderly and children. That was all her. I had given her no credit for her generosity.

"This is the contract you had written." He handed me the dusty paper. I read the contract. Glimpses of my emotions coming back to me. The feelings of excitement that I solved a problem, the hope of a new future. I knew I had written it. It didn't seem real. Felt like a dream again. Something just out of reach.

"Do you have the other one as well?"

"Yes." He pulled the second scroll that was ripped in half out of the box. I placed them together, at the bottom my signature was clearly scribed. I began reading again. My stomach sick with anxiety. It was a slave contract. I would never sign a contract like this even if I hated the person. I felt the anger towards Erebos swell up inside me again. I thought I should go back and kill him for his treachery.

Gregory put his hand on my shoulder. "When you pleaded with her to sign the contract, I saw her heart break in two. I know she took something from you. I saw her mumble the words. That's when you no longer knew her. When she left, Erebos was up in arms. He instilled fear into most of the council members. All our signatures were on that document. Erebos convinced us all she would retaliate against us. It wasn't until she appeared again to ask for our help in the war that I realized Erebos was a liar. He had been manipulating all of us for his bidding. We in turn did her a huge injustice by listening to him. Now that you know the truth. What are you going to do?"

"I don't know. What can I do? I have responsibilities. It's not like I can end our traditions and start over."

"But, that's exactly what you should do. You told me once you were bound to this girl. You proved that in your contractual proposal. Now, you choose not to make an effort. You have every right to end this tradition."

"No, I will not throw away a chance with one of these other women I do love at a possibility that my not exist anymore. I've changed. I am different."

"You are different. You are not the person I knew."

I handed him back the contracts and left. I no longer wanted to talk to him. I was angry. Angry at him. Angry at myself. Angry that he may be right. I headed to Sanna's. It was getting late, I wanted to talk with her.

Going to Sanna's was a bigger mistake. She was as stubborn as Gregory was. Her and Ethan both ganging up on me. They didn't get the complication I was in. It was easier to not see Raina and not find out more than it was to end my relationship with Lace or stop the process. I wasn't convinced that Raina was the right decision. I still loved Lace.

After last night, talking with Raina. I was now more confused than ever. I went to the village square where my mother would be arriving by coach. I hoped she could give me some good advice. The coach arrived on time and after a welcome greeting, we walked back to my home.

"What's troubling you son?"

"I don't know what to do?"

"Your father was the same way. Torn by feelings that changed in the competition."

"It's not just that. There is something else to. Can we wait till we get home first? I don't want any gossip spreading through the market. I have enough troubles as it is."

We made it home, I got her set up in my spare room. Her interviews were to start in an hour so I had little time to talk.

"Mom, when you went through the competition, Dad had his own nominee right?"

"Yes, I wasn't even on his radar. It was when the games were over and we had the dance to start the final three. He had danced with Carmen, his nominee. From the looks of it, they were in love. As the night went on, I waited. I didn't want to be caught in the competition on the dance floor. I liked your father, but I only knew him in passing."

"So did he finally ask you to dance?"

With a laugh, "He did. It was the last song of the night. As we danced, he said nothing. He didn't even look at me. When it was over, left without a word. I was horrified. I thought he hated me."

"But he loved you."

"Yes, he did. He was fighting his wolf. Our inner bond was instant. It was his emotions he struggled with. He felt obligated to Carmen, but was attracted to me. As the events took place, he found himself hoping I would make it, not Carmen, even though he told her he loved her."

"How did he know you were the one, besides you winning?"

"He listened to his instincts. They led him to his true feelings and when I was announced the winner, he allowed himself to forget his vow to Carmen to become mine. Best decision of his life." She added with a smile.

"What if my instincts are pulling me to more than one women?"

"Oh, that is a problem. Your instincts should only pick out the one scent that is a match to you."

"Maybe that's the problem, they all smell the same to me."

"That is a problem. Are your sinus's okay?" She grabbed my face and began pushing my nostrils wide and opening my mouth to look down my throat. I batted her hands away. "I'm fine mother."

"Then their must be another explanation."

"Yeah, but what, and what do I do in the mean time."

"I would spend as much time with them as you can. Try to work it out."

"Fine and dandy, but when do I have the time?"

"This is important son, you must make time."

"Who are you seeing first, maybe I can spend time with the other one during your interview."

"Lace is first."

"Well, that won't work, I don't know where Pearl is staying. I can't seem to find her unless it's at a challenge."

"Interesting? Pearl is next and the third, Teela, she is last, you could go see her now."

"Why would I see her?"

"You said more than one. I assumed it was all three women."

"It is three women, but one is not in the competition."

"Why not?"

"I .. It's a long story, but I told her to leave Ladow and not come back."

"Yet you have feelings for her?"

"I did once, now not so much, but I am drawn to her like the others."

"Well, maybe I can help. You can listen in on our conversations from the other room. Hopefully their answers will add some clarity to your situation."

"I don't know if I should."

"Nonsense. There is nothing wrong with it. Fact is your father did that as well. Now when is Sanna coming over?"

"She should be here any second…"

The door flew open and Sanna ran to our mother for an embrace. They gushed over one another then went about getting caught up on Sasha and Ethan. They were having a great time. Sanna turned to me. "I need to speak to mom alone, can you leave for twenty minutes?"

"Twenty minutes, but the interviews start in ten, mom!"

"Son, let us be. We will figure something else out to help you."

I stomped out the door. I wanted to hear the interviews. I wanted help easing the turmoil in my mind. I may not be able to hear Lace's interview, but I could still sneak back in before Pearl's I thought. At that, I strolled off toward the market.

Interview
Raina

Today I was meeting Balera. Leon and Sanna's mother. Sanna said I had nothing to worry about. I was still anxious. Our meeting was late in the afternoon. I had all morning to think about it. Sanna talked me into staying again when I returned early this morning. I wanted to hope it wasn't goodbye. Now, with both of them out for the day, I had nothing to do but sit around an empty house all by myself. I cleaned everything I could which only took an hour. I still had hours to go. I found some old books and decided reading might pass the time faster than watching the empty fireplace.

I had read the same paragraph now for an hour. Nothing was calming my mind. I went and changed my outfit again for the fifth time. It was less than an hour till I needed to head out. I opted for a soft turquoise green short sleeved shirt and a short white skirt allowing the breezes to cool my legs. I knew the scars would be hidden in my rouse, so I wasn't as self conscious as I normally was. My feet I clad in a soft leather sandal. It was going to be a hot day. I was happy with my pick. The colors made my eyes shine and my skin look soft. One last twirl in the mirror and I was ready to go. If I walked slow enough, I would be there right on time. I put my disguise in place and left the house.

I didn't walk slow enough, because I could see the edge of Leon's home, time indicated I was twenty minutes early. What to do now, I thought. She may not be there. She may be with another person. She might be eating. I was letting my anxiety make me crazy. I decided to loop around the house and head to the meadow then back. That should fill my time. As I came up to the back of his home I could hear Lace. I couldn't tell what she was saying, only that it was in anger. I could hear her stomp down the stairs. She turned on my side of the house. We were face to face.

"She's evil!" Lace yelled at me. "Watch out. You have no chance with a witch like her."

I didn't know what to say. Instead I moved to the side so Lace could continue stomping away. As she passed me, she rammed her shoulder into my arm pushing me onto the wood siding of the house. It scratched my palms causing them to sting and bleed. I waited for her to be out of view, then walked around the house holding my hands up and blowing on them to stop the stinging.

"Are you Pearl?" I heard a voice say, and looked up at the open doorway. There standing on the porch was an older women. She looked like Sanna. A smile passed across my face. If Sanna was twenty years older they would be twins.

"Yes, I'm Pearl. I'm sorry I am early, I would be happy to come back closer to my time."

"No, come in, are you hurt?"

"Small scrape. Nothing a little water won't fix."

"Come in. We can take care of that."

I walked up the steps of the porch. She waved me in. As I walked through the door, I felt the mirage of magic melt away. I stopped in a panic. Pearl was gone. There was no way to hide it.

"So, I see you have a secret?" The older woman said.

"I can explain. I know this doesn't look good, but if you let me explain."

I couldn't read her face. It was the look Leon gave me after our dances. She waved me to the sink. There turned on the water. Taking my hands gently washed them of the debris. She looked at my arms then back down to my hands. Patting them dry asked, "Explain." She said in an even tone.

I took a deep breath then sat in a chair in the kitchen. She passed me a drink, I took a sip then began to tell my story. How I met him. Why I was back. Why Pearl.

She listened quietly. Her face still holding no emotion. I finished my story. Sat patiently waiting for her to speak. As I did I noticed the draped talisman across the bow of the front door. She had diffused the magic on purpose. I jumped back to attention when she cleared her throat.

"Why do you love him?"

"I didn't say that I did."

"Your story says otherwise."

"I don't know exactly. I guess it's because he is kind, and protective. He loves his people. He has a good heart."

"And what of his position?"

"I know he is chief, but to me he is Leon. I would hope I would give him the support he needs to continue to do his job. The people need him as much as he needs them."

"What will you do in your responsibilities to the village as wife of the chief?"

"I never really thought about it. Honestly, I don't know that he would have me even if I did win. He may decide I am not for him."

"If he did claim you, then what?"

"If I were to be his wife, I guess I would do what I could to protect and help the people of this land. I don't know what I could offer, or that I have any skills of worth but I would do my best, hopefully learn from those around me."

"You think you are the best fit for my son?"

"I think only Leon knows that answer. I only want what's best for him, and if it's not me, as long as he is happy, that is all that matters."

"What will you do when this is over and you are not chosen?"

"I will return to my homeland."

She looked me over. Her eyes moving slowly from my head to my toes and then back again. I felt stripped of my clothing. As if I were on display, every imperfection spotlighted. It was unnerving. She finished her observation and stood. Then walking to the door, opened it wide. I took the cue it was time for me to leave. I walked out the door. As I did, she spoke quietly, "Don't forget your disguise my dear." I realized I hadn't tried to put it back in place, but then I wouldn't be able to until I left. Sitting in that room I knew what little magic I could do would have no affect there. I stepped out door and put my mirage in place than continued down the steps and onto the path back to Sanna's.

Discovery
Leon

I was running late, but with luck, Pearl would not be there yet. I rounded the corner in time to see Raina walk out of my house. Then in a blink of an eye, Pearl appeared before me. I rubbed my eyes. It was definitively Pearl walking down the path. I ran up the stairs and stared at my mother.

"One mystery solved son."

"You knew?"

"I'm your mother of course I knew."

"Are they really the same person?" I was flabbergasted. She was tricking me again. Now I could only feel anger for them both. Why would she trick me this way? I was just starting to let my guard down, now this. I knew I shouldn't have trusted her. I began pacing behind the chairs. "Why would she deceive me? Now I'll never trust her. She would surely know that, yet still she did it."

"Sit!" My mom ordered. I came around the chair and sat facing her. My anger now boiling over.

"Are you mad that she deceived you, or are you mad that one of them does not exist?"

"Both!" I yelled back. "She had her chance, I wanted to move on. Here I find out that I had feelings for someone that doesn't exist. How am I supposed to feel? At least I have my answers. I knew I shouldn't have doubted Lace."

"Ohh, don't you get me started on that one. She is more deceitful than you know. She has tainted you worse than anything Pearl or Raina has done. Why did you not tell me about Raina?"

"She didn't matter. She doesn't matter."

"I think she does."

"No, you don't know her. She stole my memories. She changed who I was. You can't trust someone like that."

"Do you think if she showed up to the games as herself, you or others in the village would allow it? Would show her no prejudice or discrimination for who she is?"

"That's not the point!"

"Isn't it son. Did you not ask her to leave."

"My point exactly, who would stick around when they are unwanted."

"You are as stubborn as your father. A pigheaded fool. You are not seeing what is happening here."

"What is happening here?"

"Leon, you need to give into your instincts. Let them guide you. You are letting your anger cloud your emotions. Let it go."

"Easy for you to say, she didn't play with your emotions."

"No, she didn't she was honest and thoughtful. She is a good match for you. She still loves you. I am proud she has the courage to fight for you even though you have rejected her time and time again."

"Isn't that my instincts talking? If I keep rejecting her, then it is over. Done. She should leave."

"You fool. If you truly rejected her, had no connection with her at all, you would not keep going back to her. Do you do that with anyone else?"

"Yes, Lace and I have a strong connection with her."

"Son, you are the only one deceiving yourself. Raina, Pearl, whatever you want to call her, may have a mask on the outside, but she is true to her soul. You are the one playing tricks." She held up her hand to stop my comments from coming and walked out the door. She sat on the porch looking out over the trees. I needed to get out here. I didn't like arguing with my mother. I didn't like anything she had said. She didn't get it.

I found myself at the arena. They had dismantled the dome ceiling opening it up to the sky above. Just past the large white carved doors was now a maze of green ivy hedges filled with soft white flowers. The maze looked as if it extended past the arena into the woods beyond. The walls and far side of the arena no longer existing. There was still lots to be done. I began helping with the preparations. It would get my mind off Raina and my mother. I could still feel my anger. A few times I was asked to work on another project, I was destroying the delicate flowers. It was true, I had a pile of petals at my feet.

By the time night fell, the arena had been completely transformed. I on the other hand had not. I was still heated with anger. I walked the path towards my home. Half way there I came across Lace. She was waiting in the path.

"Lace?"

"Leon, there you are. I needed to talk with you. I heard you may be out this way."

"What is it, what's wrong?"

"I don't want to speak ill of a loved one, but I know Sanna has turned your mother against me."

"What are you talking about?"

"That's why I'm here. I needed to tell you my side before they tried to turn you against me."

"Why would they do that?"

"You know Sanna doesn't like me. Well, she was with your mother when I arrived. From the start she was throwing accusations at me. I only want what's best for us. You mean everything to me. I love you Leon."

She threw her arms around my head and was leaning her body on mine. Her eyes began to swell with tears. She buried her face in my chest.

"Oh Leon, what are we to do?"

"Calm down. Now tell me what happened?"

"I told you. I arrived at your home and Sanna answered the door. She insulted me before I could even say hello. Who knows what lies she told your mother about me. Then, your mother called me a thief and liar. Oh, Leon, what ever shall we do. You do love me don't you."

"Of course I do. Why would she call you a thief?"

"I don't know! The only thing I've stolen is your heart I hope."

"That makes no sense."

"But its true. Then she said I don't love you. How can she say that? You know I do don't you."

"Yes, I do. Are you sure you didn't misinterpret her comments."

"No! Are you taking her side? Are you agreeing with her that I don't love you? I'm a thief and a liar?"

"Wo, that's not what I said. It just doesn't sound like my mom."

"That's because Sanna did this. She said things to her. How can I defend myself against your sister?"

"Look, I know Sanna has her differences with you, but she wouldn't sabotage your interview. I will have a talk with them."

"So you think I am over reacting, lying."

"No, I just think there was a misunderstood with you all. We can easily clear it up. You'll see."

"You don't love me. You don't trust me."

"Lace, what would you have me do?"

"Take my side for once. Stand up for me. You know me. You know I love you. That should be enough for you to trust me. Know I am right."

"Lace, this is my family. I need to talk things out with them."

"So, you're not on my side. Why am I even trying to be your wife when you don't love me."

"What, you sound like you would have me choose. My family or you?"

"Yes! If you want to prove your love you will choose me this time."

"Lace?"

"Me or them?"

"Lace, I can't make that choice."

"You would choose them over your feelings for me. Our bond. Our connection. Our love. I'm hurt."

"Lace. I do choose you. I will let them know they were in the wrong to make you feel this way. To question your love and nature. How does that sound?"

"Leon, I would appreciate that. They just made me out to be this monster. You know I am not."

"No, you're not Lace."

She leaned in and kissed me. Then with a smile on her face left for her home. I wasn't sure what she was talking about, but the words my mother spoke earlier entered my mind, 'she is more deceitful then you know.'

I headed home, now more frustrated than ever. My mother was cooking dinner over the stove. She waved me to a chair in the kitchen. "Mom, we need to talk."

She poured me a bowl of stew and sat across from me. "Whenever your ready." She announced.

"What happened in your interview with Lace?"

"Oh her. Not what I thought we would talk about but okay. Let's see. She said she loved you. Was devoted to you. Couldn't wait to be in control. Nothing much. Very nice girl."

"Really, that's not the story she told me."

"Oh, I see."

"What do you see, Mom, I love this woman! You have to be kind to her."

"I gave her the kindness she deserved."

"Mom, that doesn't mean much. You don't even know her."

"I knew enough."

"Yeah, from Sanna. She never liked Lace. You shouldn't have let her persuade your opinion."

"Sanna didn't say anything about Lace. She was leaving as Lace arrived."

"Well, she did say something to Lace. It really upset her."

"If she did, I didn't hear it."

"So, you say Sanna didn't try to convince you Lace was not the right choice for me."

"Yes, that is what I am saying, Sanna and I never discussed Lace in the slightest."

"Then why would Lace come away thinking you disliked her. You thought she was a thief and liar?"

"I don't know, maybe it was something she said. Maybe she's mad at herself for letting her true feelings come out."

"What did you do?"

"I didn't do anything. I let the serum do all the work. I sat quietly and listened."

"What serum?"

"The truth serum I gave to all the contestants. It's the only way to know for sure their true intentions with you son. Come now, don't look at me like that, your grandmother did it to me."

"That's not the point. You can't do that."

"Son, are you troubled that she may not be who she seems?"

"No! I know who she is."

"Great, that's settled, no need to discuss it further."

She was done with her meal, rinsed her bowl and went to the fireplace. "Mom. Why would you do that?"

"You asked for answers, I wanted you to know what was truth and what was not."

"I love her."

"You told me you loved more than one women when I arrived. Has that really changed?"

"Yes. I can't forgive someone who blatantly deceived me?"

"You need to look at why. What is she trying to prove?"

"How do I know that?"

"You ask."

"How can I believe them, her?"

"Trust your instincts. They will tell you. I've had a busy day, so I will see you in the morning for the challenge. Meet you there."

"Good night mom."

"Good luck son, and if I might suggest, no jewelry in tomorrows event. Wouldn't want any of our contestants to loose something so valuable."

I dismissed the thought, my focus on game tomorrow. I cleaned the dishes then laid down for the night. My mind kept replaying conversations over in my mind. Lace, Raina, Pearl.

I woke early. I needed to stop the lies, stop the deceits. I had a plan. I dressed and headed to the arena early to put my plans in place.

Labyrinth
Raina

When I saw Sanna that evening, she was nothing but smiles. "I'm glad my mom knows. She likes you ya know."

"I wasn't sure. I got the impression she didn't."

"That's just her. She told me everything. You were the highlight of the interviews. She's cheering for you also."

"So, she's okay with Pearl?"

"Yeah, I explained it was my idea. She gave us props for being so creative. That and the fact you look like my grandmother."

"What? You did that on purpose."

"Yeah I did. Thought Leon would pick it up by now. Funny. My mom caught it right off the bat. She didn't need any talismans to know you were in a disguise."

"I could hit you right now."

"Aw, but you love me."

"Yeah, I do. You are the best sister anyone could ask for."

"I know it."

We hugged and giggled some more. Ethan just rolled his eyes and went to his room. "Call me when supper's ready." He yelled out. We went to work preparing dinner, the rest of the evening uneventful.

Morning came. We all headed out to the arena together. At the participants entrance we said our good-byes. They headed up the flight of stairs to the seating area. I waited in the white room behind the beautiful white carved doors. The others had not arrived yet.

We were all here and the official gave us the rules. They were simple. Make the right decisions to exit the maze. You will be rewarded on your ethics and speed. Okay, it was oddly phrased, but the goal was to get to the end fast.

The official then held a bag up to each of us. Please remove your jewelry. I was the only one not wearing any. In turn, he gave each of us a wooden talisman to wear. I looked at the engraved markings on the block of wood. I could feel my magic hum. My mask was still in place. He didn't explain what it was for, only that we were to keep it on at all times. Leon walked into the room then.

He collected the bag from the official and wished us all good luck.

The doors opened wide and the three of us entered the arena. It was transformed into a green and white garden. The walls of ivy stretched high above our heads. In the sky, our bodies illuminated. I lifted my hand, and my mirror above did the same. The talisman was a transmitter of our actions and moves. I got it. We were each introduced, the crowd energetic and anxious. I could feel their energy making me eager to begin. We lined up at the opening of the maze. To my far left I could see the exit. A beautiful wood carved frame with symbols outlined the opening we would exit. I thought to myself, that at some point this labyrinth would circle back. I would need to orient myself to that fact.

A bell rang. The race began. Teela and Lace transformed and ran ahead. I took off running. The crowd went wild. They were out of my site with in a few turns. I looked above my head and could see them further into the maze. I needed to be strategic. I couldn't just hope I took all the right turns. I made my first turn then a second. Then hit my first crossroad. I plucked flowers from the wall and left an arrow of direction for future reference if needed. It was smart to do, because I hit my first dead end and had to back track. Getting back to the flowers, changed the marking and continued on. Turn after turn, backtracking and re-tracking. I was getting close to the middle of the maze. I rounded a corner and hit a crossroads to one end I could hear the soft whimper of a young cub.

I could ignore it, turn down the other path instead. I felt compelled to follow the noise. It led me to a young wolf cub. No older than Sasha when I first met her. Scared of the commotion, it had coward into a corner. I sat on the ground and waited for it to come to me. I knew it would cost me time, but it needed help. I didn't see anyone else there.

I looked up at the sky. My mouth was moving, but no sound came out. The crowd could only see me, not hear me I summarized. I continued to wait talking to the pup. It began crawling slowly to me. I picked it up and held it in my arms. It was shaking. Softly I reassured it that we would find its family. I took it with me. Following my marks, I ran back to the start line. As I approached the opening the young pup jumped out of my arms and ran to the white doors. I watched as a pair of loving arms picked it up and welcomed it home.

I couldn't stay and watch, I knew I was further behind. I ran back to the middle crossroad I had detoured, the markers aiding me along the way. I discovered a few more wrong turns, then hit a streak of what appeared to be right. I came around the corner and saw Teela trapped by a Ankylynx. It was on the defensive. I stopped in my tracks. The Ankylynx seeing my approach turned its anger on me. I was just the right distraction for Teela to get away. Now, what was I to do.

I remembered the song. It soothed the beasts. I began singing. It continued to growl and stalk me. I followed it movements, keeping my movements slow and singing all the while. The cat snapped out one last growl, then laid on his back and rolled around. I walked up to the cat, continued singing. Began stroking its stomach. I could hear the soft purr noises it was making. I looked around the corner, Teela was long gone. I looked behind me, I could see Lace creeping by. I stayed were I was singing and stroking the cat till she passed. When she was out of site, I gave the cat one last stroke, stood and slowly walked away. Singing my song till I was out of site.

At least I knew where the others were. I thought I was farther behind them. So to see them both was a relief. I scrambled thru a few more turns, running into Teela again. She seemed flustered. I yelled at her she was going the way we had come. Her response back, to mind my own business. I hoped she wouldn't meet up with the Ankylynx again. I wouldn't want to see either of them hurt.

I saw Lace come out behind a hedge. She looked at me. "Don't go that way, it's a dead end."

"Thanks"

I marked my path then ran behind her. She was moving at a slower pace. I found I could keep up with her. We came to a fork, I could see the arena doors over the hedge, I knew we were close. Right or Left. Lace turned to the right and picked up her speed. I began to follow. I heard someone yell help. Teela! She was in trouble. She yelled again. Lace stopped and we looked at each other. Then Lace took off again around the corner out of site toward the exit. I turned and ran toward the voice.

It was Teela, she took a wrong turn and found herself deep in a hole. I looked down at her. "Are you okay?"

"No, I broke my ankle when I fell. I didn't see the hole till it was to late."

"I'm coming for you."

She began crying again. I looked around. The only thing I could use was the ivy. I pulled as much as I could from the hedge. Weaved it together to give it strength. I tested the length. Just a few feet more should do it. I heard the crowd burst into cheer. I looked up and saw Lace cross the finish line. She was first. I looked down at Teela.

"Go, finish the race she said."

"No, we will finish together. You and me." I winked at her. Teela's tears faded for a moment and she smiled back at me.

I wrapped the vine around my waist then lowered the rest down the hole. "Okay, tie it around your waist and I will pull you up. You will have to use your good foot and hands to climb the walls. I don't think I can lift you completely. Got it"

"I'll try."

I watched as she stood on her good leg and hopped to the edge closest to me. "Ready?" I yelled. "Ready." She replied. I took a few steps back and braced my self. I could feel her weight as she left the ground. I stepped back as she reached up, pulling at the ivy. Sweat was dripping down my brow. I could finally see the tips of her fingers. Then her other hand. She had one elbow over the edge then the other. I ran to her and pulled her up the rest of the way. We untied the ivy from our waists. For a moment we sat catching our breath.

I helped her up and she put all her weight on me. We walked to the finish line. As we crossed, I felt the hum of my magic disappear. Teela looked at me with wide eyes. I tried to put my mask back up, but it was to late. Teela backed away from me horror stricken. The crowd gasped at my reveal. I searched behind me. Hanging on the exit door the same talisman from the other day at his home. I looked at Leon who was standing by the officiator. I couldn't read his face. I looked to Sanna, she was horrified. She started moving down the seats and headed to the stairs. I lifted my head, straightened my back and headed to the grand entrance. I wasn't going to run. I wasn't going to cry. I made it out of the arena without crumbling. With no one around, I let my tears come.

Decision
Leon

The crowd went from stunned to anger, and began to boo or call out names. It was harsh. I watched as Raina walked out of the arena her head held high. I looked at Lace, she was stunned. She walked up to Raina and with a snicker, called her a fraud. Teela was sitting on the ground. Her ankle cradled in her lap. Her face a picture of horror and shock. I looked for Sanna, she glared at me. I could feel the anger even at this distance. My mother was sitting below her. A look of disappointment on her face. She stood and followed Sanna down the stairs to the exit.

I caught Lace moving toward me. She looked at the bag I was given. "Best you know now how manipulative she is. Good reddens to her." I looked at Lace. She was so mean. The crowd was so mean. I began to feel conflicted with my actions. I rationalized the situation to be in the best interest of everyone here. They had just as much a right to know the truth as I did.

I looked at Lace with warmth in my heart. Something seemed off. She didn't smell like Lace. She had a pine, and mulch smell to her. It was off putting like the attitude she had shown Raina. She reached for the bag I was holding. Riffled through it's contents. "Where is my necklace?" I could hear the panic in her voice. She took a few steps away from me then dumped the contents onto the ground. "Where is my necklace?" She repeated with more zeal.

"I don't know. Maybe Sanna still has it, she was admiring it earlier."

"Sanna, you let Sanna take my necklace."

"I'll get it back."

"She'll ruin it."

"Nonsense, she wouldn't do that." I took a few steps toward her. I could smell that awful stench. I took a step back.

"Until you return my belonging I don't want you near me." She ran to the exit. I thought I should follow, but didn't have the urge. She was acting like a spoiled brat. Instead I let her go, and walked to Teela. She was now with the healers. Potions and wraps were placed on her ankle. "Are you okay?"

"Yeah, I was so frazzled in the maze. If it wasn't for Pearl…I guess she's not Pearl. Do you know who she is?"

"She is Raina, the wizard."

"I've heard the stories. I shouldn't have acted the way I did. I thought of Pearl as a threat in the games. I was mean to her. Then, when she wasn't herself. I reacted, pushed her away. I know it was wrong, but the stories the scars. I don't know what to believe. She was nothing but kind to me. I should apologize, I judged her without knowing her."

I could feel a pang of guilt. I stood, and caught sight of my disappointed mother watching me at the exit. My guilt deepened. I walked to her.

"Sorry mom, but it had to be done. No more lies, no more deception. It needed to be stopped."

"This was not the way." She shook her head and walked away from me. I reached out to her, and she shrugged off my hand and kept walking.

This was not going how I planned. I looked around me. The ground keepers and custodians would not look me in the eye. When they did, it was with disgust. My guilt continued to grow. Members of our elite came down and congratulated me on discovering the truth. 'How dare she enter the games' 'We don't want her here.' The comments became more callus and judge mental. I couldn't shake the guilt. I had rationalized the same remarks. I was a coward, and I knew it.

The council called an emergency meeting. I was summoned to attend. I waited outside the council chambers. I could hear the mumbles of heated arguments. My mother came into the hall. She sat next to me.

"Why did you do it?"

"I had to stop all the lies, all the tricks."

"Did you feel you succeeded?"

"This is not what I wanted."

"What did you expect would happen? You confronted her in a cowardly way in front of an unforgiving crowd."

"I know, I feel bad about that."

"I don't think you do. You don't deserve her you know. She is to good for you." She rose from her seat and walked to the chamber doors. I lifted my hand to stop her. "Mom you can't go in there."

"Watch me. You may learn a thing or two about being a leader."

I was stunned by her response. It hit me to the core. I wanted to run in behind her and at the same time, crawl under the bench I was seated on. I chose to sit where I was and wait to be called.

I sat for over an hour. Then, I saw Raina be escorted by messenger to the room. She did not look at me. As she passed, the guilt and anguish I felt intensified. I felt my own betrayal to my inner wolf making me nauseous. In that moment I hated myself. I waited longer. Then Teela came in. Again being escorted by messengers. She gave me a sympathetic look then hurried into the chamber room. Last to arrive was Lace. She kept her distance from me. Looking at me from a far with daggers in her eyes. "Did you get my necklace back yet?" She called to me.

"No, I've been a bit busy." I was baffled by the question. The necklace could wait. Something bigger was happening. Didn't she get that?

"See that you do by tonight." She warned me.

She had to walk by me to get to the doors, when she did that awful stench of mulch and pine followed her. I crinkled my nose at the smell.

I waited for some time. Finally, the doors opened and I was called in. I stood at the center podium facing the council. Behind me seated was my mother, Teela, Lace, and Raina. I couldn't read my mothers face. She was the one who taught me the art of disguising your emotions. Teela and Lace looked nervous. Raina looked at her hands seated in her lap. At that moment, my guilt was so overwhelming, I wanted to go to her. Tell her I was a coward, beg her forgiveness. Make things right. For the first time since I discovered the truth, I knew what she must have felt when she took my memories. I turned to the council.

Divide
Raina

Sanna was the first to arrive back at the house. Ethan had been called as a special witness in a session with the Council. I knew I would have to end my disguise, but this. I was not prepared for this. I don't think any of us were.

"How could he do that to you?"

"We don't even know it was him."

"Yes, we do, he said he had a plan to stop the deception. I just didn't realize he would go that far."

"He did it on purpose? Are you sure?"

"Yes, that's what makes me so mad. Why not come to you directly? How could he!"

Sanna was more mad than I. I was sad. I didn't know how he found out, but it was for the best. He had told me to move on the other night when I was myself. Now, this was just his way of letting me know I was not wanted in any form. Even as Pearl.

I went to Sasha's room and began packing. Sanna followed me.

"You're leaving now?"

"Don't you think I ought to?"

"I don't know. There has to be another way. You two are meant for each other."

"I don't think we are. Maybe it's time to accept the fact that our paths were meant to only cross, not to be together."

"That can't be true."

"I think it is. Sanna, I will always think of you as my sister. I will always be here for you and the people of this village. I need to go. I need to move on. I need you to let me."

Sanna began to cry. She helped me pack my bags. I had begun to line them up at the door. Waiting for the time to leave to make the coach. Ethan had not arrived yet. I dropped my last bag when a soft knock wrapped on the door. I looked for Sanna, she was in her room. I opened the door.

"Raina, you have been summoned to the Council."

"Sanna? Sanna?" I called.

"What! What are they going to do to her?" Sanna asked the messenger.

"I don't know. I was only asked to retrieve her."

I looked at Sanna and gave her a big hug. "I will be okay. Nothing they can do that is worse than I have already been through." I gave her a half smile. It was the best I could do. I didn't even believe my own words. I looked to the messenger and together we walked in silence to the Council Chambers.

As I walked in, I could see Leon sitting on the bench. His face void of emotion. I couldn't look at him. I focused on the gentleman escorts back and followed him into the chamber.

Silence echoed in the room as I entered. The messenger faded into the shadows. Behind me seated was Balera. On the Council, I saw one friendly face, Raoul. I saw others I recognized from years ago, and the rest from the day of the Koboldrone.

"Before we begin," the Council man paused. "We need to know that you are in fact also the contestant Pearl."

"Yes, she is an illusion of my creation."

"This was your idea to deceive the people of Ladow"

"Yes, Understand, I was not trying to deceive the people. I only wanted a chance to make things right."

"A disguise? How would that help you to make things right?"

"I regretted an action I had made and wanted to try and set it right. The only way I could do that was by participating. I felt that would not have happened unless I was in disguise. Leon, would not have allowed it. Would you have?"

"No, we probably wouldn't have." Someone chimed in.

"With your gifts, it would have been unfair for anyone else. Don't you agree?" Another said.

"How do we know you didn't use them anyway?" A third asked. "She is mocking our traditions."

"How do we know you won't do something you regret now?" Still another one asked.

"We can't trust her!" The first said.

"Stop!" Raoul stood as he spoke. "You all are letting rumors and fear decide your actions. This is the same mistake the last Council made. Do we want to repeat the actions of Erebos? She has helped our village time and time again, and yet you all still do not trust her. Why?"

"She is one of them." Someone commented back.

"So you are one of them to her. Did you not think of that. She should not trust us. When have we held up our word to her?"

The room was silent. I decided I needed to address the group. "Councilmen." I paused. "Please forgive my actions. I would in no way as you say, mock your traditions. I only wanted to give Leon a chance to get back what I took, his memories. Nothing more. I can assure you that other than my illusion of appearance, I did not use any magic on any challenges. I also understand how you may feel. I am prepared to do what you want of me to atone for my actions of deceit."

I waited patiently for them to speak. When they finally did, it was to discuss their decision in private. They all stood to leave, but were stopped by Balera.

"I haven't had a chance to speak on behalf of Raina." She stated.

"Yes, Balera."

"I have had a chance to get to know this girl. I find her trustworthy and loyal to my son. So much that the rouse she had in place was necessary. I knew of this deception and did not tell you. I knew and did not tell my son. I knew and would ask her to do it again. Do you not remember all she has done for your family, friends, and loved ones. The War. The Koboldrone. Countless others from the fortress of Nezra. Have you not seen her in the games show charity and kindness. Is she not the only candidate that excelled in all the ethical tests given in your trials? Can you say that of any of the other nominees. No, you cannot. I want it noted that she should not be punished in any way and be allowed to continue as herself in the remainder of the ceremonial games."

Raoul nodded and together they turned and filed out the small door hidden behind their chairs. I stood alone at the podium with Balera standing at her seat behind me.

"Don't worry child. They'll make the right decision this time."

"I don't know about that. My experience with trusting them to do the right thing has proven to be wrong every time. I don't know that now would be any different."

"Come sit with me."

"Thank you for being nice to me."

"You have done so much for my family, I could only feel gratitude for you."

"Thank you nonetheless."

"You know, he's just confused. Doesn't know how to handle that."

"I know, he felt betrayed. I get that. I'm not mad at him."

"So you will stay?"

"No, he made it clear that he wanted to move on without me. I let Sanna talk me out if it before, but now, I know. I respect him enough to leave."

"He doesn't know what he wants. Stay."

I didn't respond. We both knew the answer. She sat with her hand on my knee giving small pats of reassurance as we waited. It took some time and when they finally returned, I couldn't tell by the expressions on their faces what the decision was. It put me on edge. I hated not having my magic. Now when I wanted to protect myself, I couldn't. I also knew I shouldn't. With my hopes dashed, I could feel my depression start to seep back in.

Raoul was the one to address me. I stood up and moved back to the podium. Balera moved to stand by me. Her hand on my lower back for support. It reminded me of my mother.

He began by rattling off all the things they had discussed doing. It varied from banishment of Ladow to imprisonment in the cells below. I cringed at the thought. Hanging my head low. Then the direction changed. A reminder of the help I gave. One by one they stood telling me of a story about someone I had helped or rescued that they knew or loved. I hadn't realized I had done so much.

When they had finished, the decision was given. The group decided no punishment would be given for my deception. As a curtesy I should inform the Council of my intentions and requests if I come to the village in the future. As for the ceremonial challenges. If I could convince a majority that magic was not used, I could continue to participate with the remaining two contestants. I looked at the group.

"Not necessary, I will leave first thing in the morning. I elect to withdraw from the competition."

"Hosh Posh! She is confused. Tell them you did not use magic." Balera informed me. I looked at her with surprise and confusion.

"Balera what are you doing. I'm not staying."

"You will stay. You are both being foolish. Someone has to be the voice of reason. So you will stay and compete, or I will force you to."

I knew now where Sanna got her forceful nature from. I realized as she smiled at me with a sincerity I only saw from my mom that she was doing what she thought was best for me too. I turned back to the Council.

"All I have is my word that I did not." I said to no one special.

"I believe her." Raoul chimed in.

"As do I." Gregory sounded.

"I"

"I"

The I's continued till the room was divided. From next to me, I heard another I. Balera gave her vote.

"You are not a Council member and therefore have no vote Balera." Someone said.

"I am here and you need a tie breaker, so consider me speaking on behalf of my son."

"Balera, that's not how it works."

"I am mother to the Chief. I get a vote."

With them counting Balera, the I's had it. I was granted permission to continue. Raoul nodded his head and smiled. "Raina, you will participate in the next round of challenges as yourself without the use of any magic. Understand?"

"Yes, thank you all for your kindness and understanding."

I didn't know what to do then. No one was moving. Was I supposed to leave now? I looked to Balera, she stood firm. I looked back at the Council. Raoul spoke again. "As the one who is wronged, you have the right to decide the punishment of Leon as Chief."

"No! No! I do not wish any punishment for him. I understand why he did it. I forgive him for it. Nothing more is needed in my eyes."

"This is your answer?"

"Yes."

"As a participant, you need to understand he will be removed as Chief and will no longer be bound to the traditions of the contest. Do you still wish to continue forward with the challenges?"

"Yes, I would. I would ask that you not take his birthright away from him. This is a mistake that was made to me. I do not wish to see this recourse on an action I have forgiven."

Balera spoke up then. I could feel the heat of anger coming off her skin. See the surprised look on her face as she stared at the council.

"You have no right to take away his birthright. I know you don't all feel that this mistake warrants that grand a response. It must be an unanimous vote. I will seek the votes of the people to have him reinstated as Chief." I could hear the desperation seep into her voice. She was stopped by a Councilman

"Balera! We will continue to discuss this and take all the participants remarks, as well as yours, into consideration before we have a final vote. If you will follow us, we will discuss this more thoroughly."

I watched as they all left again out the small back door. Balera moved with them. I went and sat in the chair I used before. Waiting. Soon the small door opened returning all the Councilmen and Balera. I stayed seated. Balera moved to sit by me. She patted my knee again. Her face expressionless. We watched as Teela was brought into the room and stood at the podium.

orward
Leon

"Leon we have reviewed the facts. What you did was unbecoming of a leader in our community. We have been embarrassed and shamed because of your actions. We are not happy with your lack of judgement. If the council had it's way we would remove you as chief of the village immediately."

I knew they were not pleased. I had embarrassed us all with my actions. But this, this was an unfair call. Strip me of my birthright for a mistake.

"You can't do that?" I started to gasp out. The councilor held up his hand silencing me.

"It is not our decision to make."

I held my breath. If not their decision then who's?

"We have heard from the women your actions have hurt. They voted one to allow you to stay in your position. One to have you removed immediately. One abstained from the vote. Two have chosen to decline their nomination as a contestant. With that being said the remaining women will move on to the last and final phase. We will take a final vote to decide your fate."

I watched as Gregory read the charges and put the council to a vote. One by one each member cast his vote. It was four to six in favor of me staying on as leader.

"Leon, I hope you will learn from your actions and understand we will not tolerate any additional embarrassments like the one you did today."

"I will do my best to do my duty to the people of this village." I recited the beginning of my oath. The Council members stood and exited the room. I waited for the women to leave also. It was just my mother and I left. She walked to me and put her hand on my shoulder.

"You really screwed up this time."

"I thought I was in the right when I did it. As soon as it happened, I have regretted it ever since."

"Reminds me of someone else. Maybe it's time you forgave her."

"Maybe."

"Leon, I know your confused. You need to trust your instincts on this."

"Mom, I need to be alone."

"Okay, I love you son. I'll see you at home."

She left me with my thoughts. I wandered out of the chambers and headed to my meadow.

I wasn't far from the meadow when I caught the scent of Raina. She was here. I moved toward the smell. I could see a partial figure behind the trees.

"Don't Go. I need to apologize to you."

"You sure do." Lace said as she turned from the shadows of the tree. "You should have been more careful with my things. And that stunt you pulled. I applaud you, but at the expense of your title."

"Lace?"

"So, do I get that apology, then maybe I'll consider putting my name back into the contest."

"Lace, what are you doing here?"

"I had to get my necklace." She held it up for me to see. "You weren't in any hurry to help me."

I stepped closer. She was back to her pleasant smell. I reached out and examined her necklace in my hand. Trust my instincts I thought of my mothers words.

"Lace, I won't be mad, please tell me the truth, what was your vote?"

She stumbled and tried to step back. I reached out with my other arm and gently held her in place. "Lace." I think I knew the answer, but wanted to hear it from her.

"You know they were going to strip you of your birthright. I had to agree with them. You understand. Then to save myself the embarrassment of competing for someone no longer worthy I backed out. But, that has changed. They let you stay. I already sent word to be reinstated as your nominee. Everything will be back to normal. Don't you see I did what I did because I love you."

I felt sick. My mother was right again. I was the fool. I was blinded by her scent that I didn't see the game she was playing. She wanted the title, the power, not the person. I looked down at the pendant still in my hand, trusting I was doing the right thing this time, snapped it from her neck and crushed it against the trunk of a tree. Lace was horrified. The scent that was so pleasant and attractive instantly turned to rotting mulch.

"You, why did you do this." I asked.

"You hated her, yet you pined over her. I gave you the best of both worlds. Your wolf was happy, and you were happy. You can't blame me for that."

"You tricked me."

"You let yourself be tricked."

"I could have liked you for you."

"No, you didn't. I had met you over a dozen times, and you didn't give me the time of day, so when I heard of the necklace, I stole it, and you see, here we are a perfect match."

"We are not a match. You are a liar and thief."

"No more than your precious Raina."

"You are nothing like her." I wanted to say more, but an odd smell filled the shadows of the trees. "Do you smell that?"

"I love you Leon, and I did this for you."

"Lace, enough, do you smell that?" It was getting stronger. I looked around. Lace stopped talking. She moved away from me. I could hear her struggle, I looked back at Lace. She was fighting invisible arms. Her mouth muffled.

"Lace!"

I could hear a cackle of a laugh. Then, I was thrown to the ground. I could feel the constraints and weight pressing me down. I couldn't see anything. Lace was still struggling against the air around her, and I was doing the same. I howled for aid hoping someone would come.

I continued to struggle, I could hear the panting and felt something wet drip onto my face. I managed to loosen an arm. I swung as hard as I could at the air where the wetness had come. I made contact. I heard the whimper and then a growl as my arm was pinned back to the ground again. I howled again for aid.

I heard Ethan respond. He was close. Far off in the distance I heard Thibault answer my call.

"What ever you are, they will be here soon."

"More for the slaughter I see. Then we should wait, let you watch your friends be killed."

I knew that voice, but from where. I continued to struggle. I could hear the branches breaking and out of the woods was Ethan, with Raina on his back. She slid to his side. Ethan looked around, confused at the site. Raina was poised with daggers in her hand. "Raina, I don't see anything." Ethan whispered to her.

"Can you smell them. One to our right, Two to our left holding Leon, and one behind Lace." Raina said, not taking her eyes off Lace.

"Ah, I see the tramp has eluded death and found her way here." The voice cackled.

"I see your still the coward you are." Raina responded. I could only watch. Ethan was sniffing the air and had circled behind Raina. The conversation between them continued.

"I should have killed you the first time."

"You really think you have the skills. I let you capture me. Don't think I'll be this easy on you this time."

A ferocious growl echoed around us. Lace was thrown to the ground. I watched as Raina ran towards the sound, slid on her legs, ducking under an imaginary line, then climbing onto an invisible form. Her daggers digging deep, and disappearing into thin air. The growl that followed was deafening. She was being tossed to and fro in the air. Then, the beast of a man appeared.

It was Hagar. He reached and caught hold of her shoulder ripping her from his back. She landed in a roll jumping back on her feet. Ethan was now snapping at the air behind her. Hagar was twisting to remove her other blade. She turned to face Ethan and then rounded on him and swiped with her dagger. One of Hagar's lackey's appeared before her. Ethan jumped as she ducked and attacked the wolf.

Hagar had released the knife from his shoulder blade. I could see the pools of blood spreading out over his back. Lace was huddled in a nook of a tree. Raina was motioning to her to go. She finally took the hint and transforming on the run sprinted out of the woods.

Hagar looked at her than leaned against a tree. "You think I'm at a disadvantage don't you."

"I know you are."

"Maybe I can change your mind. I only need one of you." He let out a short high whistle. Behind a tree came Mutt with something over his shoulder. He threw the item to the ground. It grunted in response, then rolled to face us. Sanna was bound and gagged. Ethan growled in anger. I could feel my own anger surface.

"Still feel you have the advantage."

"Yes, now you have a choice, surrender and let her go, or, well, let's just say, I will let these two decide."

Hagar laughed. He stood up straight. Raina looked from me to him. I knew what she wanted. I stopped struggling and instead set my sites on Hagar. He moved toward Raina. Raina moved toward constraints holding me. Ethan leapt at Mutt. In a scuffle of dirt and wind. I saw the other two appear. I transformed and lunged at Hagar, knocking him down before he reached Raina.

Hagar and I were now dancing. Snapping our jaws at one another. I heard Thibault call. I responded. It was a matter of time before they would be out numbered. He could help Raina and Ethan.

Hagar attacked. I beat him off, snapping at his neck and legs. Our battle began. We hadn't been fighting long when reinforcements arrived. I heard the battles around me intensify. Hagar watched in anger as his gang was being subdued. He turned and ran at Raina, another fierce growl echoing. He leaped, but she moved at the last second, and he missed her skidding to a stop. "You can't catch me." She taunted him. Then took off running deeper into the woods. I ran between them. Hagar charged, knocking me to the side in his pursuit of Raina.

My instincts kicked in again, I had to protect her. I got to my feet and chased after them. I could see her ahead. Hagar was gaining on her. She scrambled up a tree, barely missing the powerful snap of his jaw breaking the branch below her. I leapt onto his back, baring my teeth into the back of his neck. He howled in pain. Then began thrashing me about. I fell to the ground, but quickly got back to my feet. I looked at Raina, she was moving about in the tree, but safe. She called out, "Last chance to surrender beast."

"I will kill you both." He snarled out. I looked at him, anger in my eyes. This was a rematch I was waiting for. I took my stance and found the spot I would strike to kill him. I bared my teeth ready for the kill. Then pushed off the ground to strike. As I did, I saw her drop from the tree.

My mind was in slow motion. Her hands wrapped around her dagger. I couldn't do anything to stop myself. I was going to hit Raina, not Hagar. In the brief split of a second, we were on the ground in a pile of blood. I had attacked Raina. She lay on the ground, blood spilling from her neck. I transformed and kneeled over her. My hand trying desperately to stop the blood. I looked behind me, Hagar lay in an unmoving pile. A dagger pushed deep into his skull. Blood pooling off to the side. He was dead.

I yelled for help. She needed healing. She needed help.

"Raina, stay with me."

"I'm cold."

I removed my bloodstained shirt and wrapped it around her body carefully. Still keeping pressure on her neck.

"Raina, you can't leave me. Someone help us."

Ethan and Sanna were first to arrive. "Get help, she is bleeding to death."

Sanna took off running transforming in one leap. She would find help. Ethan limped over to me. He saw the bite from her throat. His hand went to my shoulder. "We need to move her." He removed his shirt and tore it into strips of cloth then wrapped her neck as tight as he dared. The blood was soaking through.

"Raina, stay with me." We picked her up and carried her to my home. It was the closest location to where we were. We passed the others on the way. I noticed Hagar's gang bound in a circle. We hurried.

I kicked open my door and we laid her on my bed. Robyn and my mother rushed in from outside. They went to her side. Robyn began administering lotions and chanting in an unknown tongue. My mother, handing her herbs and potions to be applied. I sat on the bed, holding her hand.

"Raina, stay with us."

She fluttered her eyes and gave me a soft smile.

"Raina, I was such a fool."

"You're not a fool." She whispered, then closed her eyes again.

Robyn and my mother exchanged glances. Then my mother stood and ushered us all out of the room. I could hear through the closed door more chanting and soft pleas for Raina to stay. I began pacing the room. Sanna was attending to Ethan's wounds. I could see her hands were shaking. A soft knock resounded on the door, Thibault let himself in.

"How is she?"

"Don't know yet. They are still working on her."

"She's a tough gal, she'll make it this time too."

"I hope your right."

"We've secured the others. I've asked Raoul to fashion some talismans for us to see past their magic. Search the woods for any stragglers lurking about."

"Good idea. Can't have any more attacks. Oh, can you send someone to check on Lace. She was there too."

"Yeah, I'll send someone right away. Anything I can do for you?"

"No, yes, send for Gregory."

"As you wish."

He left the room closing the door behind him. Sanna was sitting on Ethan's lap wrapped in his arms. "You're thinking of work now?"

"No, I'm doing what I should have done. Setting things right."

"What do you mean?"

"I remember."

"Everything?"

"Everything!"

"When, how?"

"When Raina ran up the tree, I let my instincts take over completely. Seeing Hagar, trap Raina, well, it reminded me of when I found her on the rock, surrounded by his gang. I wasn't going to let what happened then happen again. In that decision, I had a full recollection of Raina in my life."

We waited for hours in silence. Worry sketched on our faces.

My mother and Robyn came out of the room then. "She will be out for a while. The healing is slow, we hope we saved her in time. By morning we will know one way or the other."

"Can we take her home?" Sanna asked.

"She is home." I retorted.

A soft knock and an opening of the door let Gregory in. He looked at us all. "You called for me?"

"What are you doing son?"

"Fixing my mistake."

"I want the games canceled. Can you arrange this?"

"I don't understand why?"

"I will not continue the games when I have chosen my mate. Live or die, I will be with Raina."

Gregory smiled. "You made the right decision. I will enact it immediately."

I nodded my agreement and he left. My family stared at me stunned and confused. "I guess I should explain."

The group was shocked, but I could see the satisfaction of agreement in their faces.

"No need brother, we all knew you would figure it out eventually." Sanna walked over and gave me an open, loving hug. "I hope she lives so she can see I was right."

A smile crossed my lips. It was nice to have a break in the tension of our worries.

It was getting late, Raina still had no change in her healing. We all waited, watching. One by one they left for home. My mother leaving with Ethan and Sanna. Robyn was the last to leave. "You will need to watch her through the night. If she does take a turn for the worse, send word. We will come."

I closed the door behind Robyn and went straight to Raina's side. She was barely breathing. The bandages around her neck soaked in blood. I gently lifted her to change them out. I applied more of the potion Robyn had left. I could feel a spark of energy as I touched it to her neck. I watched in amazement as tiny invisible hands began stitching her muscles and veins back together.

She stirred.

"Raina?"

"Umm."

"Raina, I am so sorry for everything I did to you. Can you ever forgive me?"

"Nothing to forgive."

"Raina, I've been a tyrant and coward."

"No, never."

She fluttered open her eyes. I could see the drowsiness in them. "Raina, stay with me."

"Always."

She closed her eyes and I could hear the soft sound of her breath. It was stronger than it had been just moments ago. I looked at her neck. The bleeding was stopped. The tiny hands still sewing her together. I took another scoop of potion and applied it generously to her neck and shoulder. Then trusting my instincts spread it down her arm.

The air was electric. I could hear it pop and crackle with excitement. I watched as the bruises and scabs began shrinking in size. Old scars disappearing with each soft crackle of magic. The potions were working again. I covered her neck and gently laid her back down. I removed the blanket that covered her legs. Gently, began applying more potion to the marks and wounds on her legs. The air electrified with pops and crackles. Her skin was healing, transforming to a soft smooth surface. I pulled her other arm from the bed and lathered it. Still the same sensation.

I let her sleep. Pulling a chair next to the bed, I held her hand in mine and closed my eyes.

ream
Raina

I woke sometime in the night. I could feel the blanket of magic that was all around me. I moved my shoulder and felt the shooting pain attack my neck and arm. Yeah, wasn't going to move that side for a while. I heard the soft sound of someone sleeping. I turned my body to look. There on a chair was Leon. His arm stretch out to me. He looked so peaceful. I didn't want to disturb him. I tried to sit up, but was unsuccessful. My moving was waking my companion.

"Don't move, I can help you."

"I just want to sit up for a minute. My mouth is dry."

"I'll get you some water." He gently put his arms around me and lifted me into a seated position. He moved the pillows around to support my neck and head. Then jumped out of the room. He was back in a flash. It put a smile on my face.

"What did I do to deserve all this attention?" I joked out.

His face flushed with embarrassment. "I, we were so worried about you."

"I have a tendency to be dramatic." I smiled back.

He leaned over and kissed my forehead. "I'm so glad you're okay."

"Are we okay?" I asked. I didn't know where we stood. So many things had happened over the last day. I needed to know what he thought, felt.

"Yes, I am so sorry for how I acted and what I did to you yesterday and all those years ago. I would never want hurt you. I was a fool."

"You remember?"

"Yeah, it all came back to me in the fight."

"I'm sorry I took them in the first place. I had no right."

"You had every right. I see that now. I hurt and betrayed you. Why did you come back?"

"Because, I was wrong in my actions."

"Is that the only reason?"

"No, I still loved you."

"And do you love me now?"

"I never stopped."

He moved the cup of water from my hands and leaned in and kissed me on the lips. It was sweet and wonderful.

"Raina."

"Yes."

"I love you too."

He moved to the other side of the bed and sat on top of the blanket, then gently wrapped his arms around me. I laid my head on his shoulder and let my eyes close. In that moment I was blissfully happy.

A few days went by. My wound was healing quickly. My old scars and other wounds had disappeared to almost nothing. I could feel the tingle of magic all around me. Night had come again. I laid in Leon's bed.

I knew I was dreaming. Only the feeling was so real. I was standing on a boat being tossed by the waves. It was a big storm, with the waves crashing over the side of the boat. The wind was howling in my ears. I watched as men scurried about fastening the sails, bailing out the water. I looked out to sea. In the distance stood a dark and foreboding island. It's tall mountain peak spitting lava into the sky. The thunder and lightening yelling back. I watched this scene as we drifted closer and closer to the island. The sea clawing at the boat begging it not to venture further.

A small dingy was lowered into the rolling sea. From below deck a hooded figure was lead to the edge. They tied a rope around its waist and lowered it to the bobbing boat below. There it was tied to the bobbing craft. The wind kicked up and I saw it blow the hood off of the person.

"Mom."

I hadn't realized I yelled it out. The action, woke me and Leon from our sleep. He came running in from the other room. I was sweating from head to toe. My face flushed, and my breath heavy. My bandages wet.

"Raina, are you all right, what's wrong."

"My mother I saw my mother."

"Your magic, you have it back?"

"I don't know."

I thought for a moment. What did I want to do? I didn't know. I thought of Leon. I focused on him sitting in the other room. I opened my eyes. He still sat next to me on the bed. That didn't work. I tried a protection wall.

"See if you can touch me."

I watched as his hands traced the invisible wall between us. It worked. I let the wall down and he tumbled forward. I caught him with magic. Steadied him back in place.

"Looks like I have some, but not all."

"So now what?"

"I need to find her."

"I know, we will go together."

He reached over and pulled me into his arms. "Can we wait till morning first?"

I laughed and snuggled deeper into his arms. "Morning it is."

Sneak Peak Part 4 The Island

Victims

Leon

I was glad to be headed out. I wanted to spend time with Raina. After everything we've been through; I missed being around her. We were taking the quickest route to the seashore. First we would travel through the River Pixies' Valley. Then it would take us out of the woods and into the baron wetlands that looked out onto the old fortress. I hoped we would not run into any Raiders leftover from the war.

The first day was pleasant enough for us both. It gave us a chance to get caught up. We had a three year gap in our relationship. Rain also used the time to practice her magic. She still couldn't do much. Raina's protection walls and domes were weak and short lived. Nothing like she could do before. She was able to see shimmer of magic on an object and the likeness it was creating. She could understand most creatures in their native tongue. Her defensive spells or curses did not work. She was also still blocked from transporting.

When evening came we set up camp. It was nothing more, than a small fire and two blankets. Nestled between some trees. The cloaks we wore providing us with warmth through the night. We had no sooner started the fire when I heard a snap of a branch come from behind us. We both turned to look. We could see a silhouette amongst the trees. Raina grabbed for her daggers. I transformed into my wolf self. Both of this ready for a fight.

The silhouette didn't seem to notice us. It continued to moving forward aimlessly. Then we saw more shadows moving about. With a shrug of her shoulders she motioned for me to circle around. We would see what was going on.

She moved ever so lightly through the trees. If it weren't for her scent I would not have known she was there. We continued moving at separate angles toward the silhouettes. Hidden behind a tree, I watched as man and women moved forward. Sickening expressions of death on their faces. Their bodies bony and weak. Shriveled in clothing too big.

I could smell Raina. She was coming my direction. I transformed back to human form. She stood by me.

"Where are they from?"

"I don't know."

"Where are they going?"

"Looks like towards home."

Raina stepped out from the tree pausing in front of one of them. He stopped. His expressionless face staring through her. She waved a hand in front of him. No response. She shook his shoulders. No response. The others moving around them.

"I think their from the Koboldrone." She stated in her inspection.

"No, it can't be."

"When I first came across it, there was this town full of people just like them."

"Are you sure?"

"Yeah, almost certain. You don't think it would come back, would you?"

"Your grandfather and Robyn said it shouldn't. Best we stay on guard."

"How do we help them?"

"If they are going towards Ladow, Robyn and Raoul will do what they can to take care of them. There is nothing you or I can do."

We stood there for hours watching as thousands of people made there way towards my home. The site so surreal. When they had all passed, there was only a few hours till sunrise. I pulled her close and walked us back to the fire that had gone out hours ago. I sat on the ground and leaned against a tree. Raina curled into my arm on the ground next to me. Her cloak wrapped around her knees.

"You think they'll be okay."

"I hope so."

We didn't say more. Slowly we both nodded off to sleep. Tomorrow we would be at the edge of the forest.

LEGENDS OF THAMATURGA

© Copyright 2016, H.C. MacDonald

Rights Reserved.

This document may be downloaded for personal use; users are forbidden to reproduce, republish, redistribute, or resell any materials from this document in either machine-readable form or any other form without permission from HC MacDonald or payment of the appropriate royalty for reuse.

Made in the USA
San Bernardino, CA
18 December 2016